DISNEY · PIXAR

BRAVE

The Junior Novelization

ISBN: 978-0-7364-2912 -2

randomhouse.com/kids

Printed in the United States of America
10 9 8 7 6

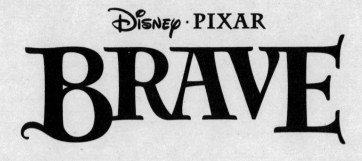

DISNEY · PIXAR

BRAVE

The Junior Novelization

Adapted by
Irene Trimble

Random House 🏠 New York

Prologue

The sun shone brightly over a green field as the long grasses bowed and danced in the wind. Although the land was wild for many leagues around, a young and happy family was set up under a tent, enjoying a carefree outdoor picnic. Several guards stood at attention nearby, for this was a royal outing. The king and queen loved their young princess, and would not risk her safety.

Not that the princess cared a fig for caution. Wild and willful, the six-year-old child raced through the field, her curly red hair streaming behind her. Then she ducked behind a rock, giggling. Her mother, the queen, pretended to gaze around innocently. Then she reached behind the rock and tickled the little girl, who popped up with a shriek of laughter. The princess was on her feet and running again, their game of hide-and-seek starting over.

The king, a large and fierce-looking man, practically blocked out the sun when he stood up. But the princess hopped excitedly around him without fear, and the king laughed when he saw her. He laid his bow and arrows on the table, and she went to stare at the weapons. Gently, she ran her fingers over the bow, awed by the carvings.

The king watched as the child tried to pick up the massive bow, its weight throwing her off balance. He wagged his finger at her, warning her to leave it be. Her look of disappointment was awful to see . . . until he pulled out another bow, full-size but lighter in weight, and a pretty white. The princess gasped delightedly. This was *her* bow!

For the rest of the day, the princess struggled with her lovely new weapon, learning to place arrows properly, working to pull the string back with enough strength. Finally, she let loose a strong shot . . . which sailed over the target and into the woods.

The princess ran into the forest, searching for the arrow. As she looked through the underbrush, she suddenly noticed a flickering blue light. The light seemed to dance through the air, sometimes bright, sometimes barely there. The princess was fascinated. Then, just as suddenly, the light vanished.

The king and queen were not far behind the princess. When they caught up, the princess told them about the blue light. The king laughed and said it was all in the girl's imagination. But the queen's eyes grew wide. The blue light was a will o' the wisp, she explained, a magical creature that could lead you to your fate. It could bring you riches or it could bring your doom.

The family did not have long to ponder the meaning of the wisp, however. With a menacing growl, a huge bear lumbered out of the woods, right in front of the princess. The creature rose to stand on its hind legs. It was gigantic— far taller than the king. The bear focused one black eye on the princess.

In an instant, the king shoved the queen and the princess out of the way and faced the huge bear. "Run!" he ordered his family.

The bear roared angrily. With its massive jaws snapping, the great beast lunged at the king, who did not flinch. Glaring, he met the bear's attack with his sword drawn— and with a roar of equal ferocity.

Long ago, when the world still brimmed with mist and magic, there lived the fierce clans of the Scottish Highlands. No one knows how these proud people came to reside in the green, windswept Highlands, and only the weathered stones of the great castles are left to tell their stories. But if those stones could talk, they'd surely tell tales of enchantment and adventure.

The stones of Castle DunBroch would have more to tell than most. One of the grandest stories begins there, long ago in the kingdom of DunBroch, when all was right with the world for a young girl named Merida.

Merida, sixteen and the princess of the realm, was being groomed by her mother to one day rise to the throne as queen. With that title came duties and responsibilities. And above all, as Queen Elinor so often pointed out, a queen had to possess grace and poise—two qualities Merida was sure her mother had been born with. That was why the queen was in charge of every single moment of Merida's day—so she could teach her daughter to become . . . her. At least, that was how Merida saw it.

But Merida didn't care about grace and poise. She liked to laugh and listen to her raucous, adventurous father, King Fergus. The round, red-bearded king was a true Highland warrior. His feats of bravery in battle were legendary. But now, in these days of peace, he had only stories of his great and glorious past.

He loved to tell how he'd lost his leg in a battle with Mor'du, the demon bear. The story had been told since Merida was a child. And to the delight of Merida and her three younger brothers, King Fergus spared none of the gory details.

Merida thought her brothers, the wild-haired triplets, Hamish, Hubert, and Harris, were lucky. In her opinion, those three got away with murder, and their only skill was running their nursemaid, Maudie, in circles. Wee devils, Merida called them.

Merida would sometimes stare out her window, which

overlooked the great blue loch of DunBroch Harbor, and sigh. She couldn't get away with anything. It seemed as though the future of the kingdom would someday depend on Merida. And so the queen pressed on with her endless lessons and high expectations.

2

Merida tried to absorb the teachings Queen Elinor doled out. One day the lesson was in public speaking. That lesson always took place in the Great Hall, where subjects gathered to hear the queen give her speeches. At one end of the huge hall were the raised thrones of Queen Elinor and King Fergus, and next to them, the smaller carved thrones for Merida and the triplets. A large stone fireplace warmed the room; above it was the crest of Clan DunBroch.

Merida stood in front of her mother's throne while Elinor stood on a balcony at the opposite side of the empty room. Merida nervously cleared her throat and began to speak. "Aye, Robin, Jolly Robin, and thou shalt know of mine." Merida looked up at her mother, hoping for her approval.

"Project!" Elinor said.

Merida swallowed and shouted, "AND THOU SHALT KNOW OF MINE!"

Elinor left the balcony and approached her daughter, shaking her head. "E-nun-ci-ate. You must be understood from anywhere in the room. Or it's all for naught!"

Merida rolled her eyes and muttered, "This *is* all for naught."

"I heard that," Elinor snapped.

Poor Merida felt there was no escape from Elinor's lessons. When Merida joined her parents for a session of falconry outside on the castle green, that turned into a lesson, too.

The queen stood elegantly, holding a hooded falcon on one gloved hand. "A princess enjoys elegant pursuits," Elinor declared as she and King Fergus released their birds.

Suddenly, Elinor's falcon flew into Fergus's face. Merida collapsed in giggles, laughing loudly as Fergus sputtered and fell to the ground.

Elinor never lost her composure. "A princess does not laugh, giggle, or chortle," she told Merida calmly. "She laughs with her eyes."

At other lessons, Elinor also insisted that Merida learn about geography and memorize the crests of all the clans. "A princess must be knowledgeable about her kingdom," she told Merida, who was sketching absentmindedly one day. Then she snatched Merida's drawing away. "She doesn't doodle!"

Even when Merida plucked the strings of her harp for fun, Elinor would sit nearby, listening carefully. "That's a C, dear," she would say, correcting Merida's playing.

Merida felt happier when she was able to let loose with her father. She and Fergus loved to exchange friendly swordplay in the courtyard. The king took great pride in his daughter's ability with a sword and a bow. She was almost as good as he had been as a young warrior. Once, during practice, Merida gave him a solid whack on his peg leg, knocking it out from under him. She danced a joyful jig as her father hit the ground.

Elinor noted the exchange. "A princess never gloats," she said as she passed them.

The next morning, at the crack of dawn, Queen Elinor cheerfully opened Merida's bed curtains and said in a lively tone, "A princess rises early!"

Merida could barely open her eyes and nod.

All day—every day, it seemed—Merida heard the same

words over and over. "A princess is compassionate. Patient. Cautious! Clean. And above all . . . perfect in every way."

That night, as always, the evening meal became a lesson. By the time the family met in the Great Hall for supper, Merida was famished. Like her brothers and her father, she jammed a handful of bread and a hunk of cheese into her mouth.

"A princess doesn't stuff her gob," Elinor said stiffly. Once again, Elinor was telling Merida what a princess must and mustn't do.

To Merida, it seemed that with every lesson, the wall between her and her mother grew. And over time, that wall came to feel as high and thick as the walls of Castle DunBroch itself.

3

To Merida's great relief, every once in a while there was a day when she didn't have to be a princess, when anything could happen and she had nothing to do but be herself. There were no lessons and no expectations.

Today was one of those days, and Merida grabbed the bow her father had given her. She raced through the castle grounds, eager to reach the stable of her beloved horse, Angus. Angus was a huge Clydesdale who stood nearly twice as tall as Merida. His soft coat was jet black except for the white on all four of his huge hooves and a patch of white between his big brown eyes.

Merida walked into Angus's stall and greeted him by hugging his huge head. She felt that they truly understood each other.

Merida happily jumped onto Angus's back and rode him full speed through the enormous castle gate. The two loved nothing more than to run free.

"Hyah!" Merida shouted, her long red hair flying in the wind as she rode over the stone bridge and into the mossy forest beyond Castle DunBroch.

Merida pulled out her bow as Angus galloped toward a collection of straw-stuffed targets that hung in the trees. She drew her bow back and—*Thunk! Thunk! Thunk!*— her arrows hit them all. Merida smiled. She never missed.

As the sun rose higher, Merida rested Angus in a shady spot. She leaned against a tree and took out her bow and knife. As she carved a Celtic symbol into the bow to help her remember this fine day, she heard an eagle cry. Merida looked up in wonder as a great golden eagle circled overhead. She took it as a sign of good things to come.

After their rest, she rode Angus farther still into the mossy forest. Finally, they reached a sheer vertical stone that stood many times taller than the towers of Castle DunBroch. According to legend, the place was called the Crone's Tooth.

Merida looked up at the steep rock face and smiled. Angus nervously took a few steps back. He seemed to sense what Merida was about to do.

4

Angus watched anxiously as Merida found notches in the rock for her hands and feet and began to climb. Hand over hand, she slowly pulled herself up to the Crone's Tooth. She stumbled occasionally as a bit of rock crumbled beneath her feet, but she never lost her grip.

As Merida climbed higher, she could see the Highlands and DunBroch Harbor below her. But when she reached the top of the rock, she saw that it was not just its height that made it the stuff of legend. As the sun passed over the mountains, a shaft of sunlight hit the waterfall next to the Crone's Tooth. To Merida's delight, it turned the waterfall the color of gold!

Merida gasped at the extraordinary beauty of the falls.

She cupped her hands and drank, then shouted down to Angus in triumphant joy. This was the Fire Falls she'd heard about in ancient stories and songs.

But after gazing at the view for some time, Merida realized that the sun was setting and she needed to return home. The family would be having their evening meal in the Great Hall, and her presence was expected.

Merida rode through the gates and past the village within the castle walls. She hopped off Angus and returned him to his stall. "I'm starving! You too?" she asked him. Before heading into the castle, she fetched him a bucket of oats.

Then, still excited from her adventure, Merida slung her bow over her shoulder and entered the castle through the kitchen door. She snatched a few fresh muffins and biscuits that had been laid out on the long kitchen table. Taking a big bite from one of the muffins, she quietly climbed the stairway from the kitchen and entered the Great Hall, hoping her lateness would go unnoticed.

The family was seated around a single table in the large, round room. Merida could hear her father, King Fergus, telling a story to the triplets. Fortunately, Elinor was preoccupied with a pile of scrolls and parchments and didn't seem to notice Merida at all.

Merida quietly sat down and laid her bow on the table.

She loved hearing her father's stories, no matter how many times she'd heard them before.

The triplets stared wide-eyed as Fergus told his most famous tale. "Then, out of nowhere came the biggest bear you've ever seen! His hide was littered with the weapons of fallen warriors, his face scarred, with one dead eye!"

Fergus's story was made all the more vivid by the stuffed trophy bears that lined the Great Hall, their teeth gleaming in the torchlight. "I drew my sword," Fergus continued, "and ..."

"Whoosh!" Merida said with a sweep of her hand. "One swipe, his sword shattered, then CHOMP! Dad's leg was clean off! Down the monster's throat it went!"

The triplets gasped, horrified.

"Oh, that's my favorite part!" Fergus said, smiling.

Merida continued the story, her voice no more than a whisper. "Mor'du has never been seen since," she said as the triplets hung on her every word. "He's roaming the wilds even now, waiting for his chance to finish the job. *RAAH!*" Merida roared, raising her arms and curling her fingers into claws.

The triplets' mouths dropped open, but Fergus only shrugged. "Let 'im return," he said. "I'll finish what I guddled in the first place."

Merida smiled, ready to eat . . . when Queen Elinor suddenly declared without looking up from her papers, "A princess does not place her weapons on the table."

Merida sighed. "Oh, Mum! It's just my bow."

Queen Elinor gave her a withering look. "A princess should not *have* weapons, in my opinion."

"Och! Leave her be!" Fergus said to Elinor. "Learning to fight is essential. Even for a princess."

Merida quietly removed her bow from the table, and Elinor returned her gaze to her scrolls. "Mum, you'll never guess what I did today!" Merida said excitedly.

"Hmm?" Elinor asked from behind her papers.

"I climbed the Crone's Tooth and drank from the Fire Falls!"

Elinor didn't look up, but Fergus and the triplets were immediately impressed.

"The Fire Falls?" Fergus said, stunned. "They say only the ancient kings were brave enough to drink the fire!"

Merida beamed as Fergus gave her a wink and brushed her chin with his huge fist. Her father's praise made Merida flush with pride.

"What did you do, dear?" Elinor asked distractedly.

"Nothing, Mum," Merida replied, sure that her mother would not approve.

Elinor looked up. Her eyes strayed to Merida's plate. "Hungry, aren't we?" she said, scowling at Merida's mountain of muffins.

Merida sighed. "Mum . . ."

Suddenly, Elinor seemed very interested. "You'll get dreadful collywobbles!" she cried. "Oh, Fergus, would you look at your daughter's plate?"

Fergus continued eating from his own plate, which was stacked just as high as Merida's. "So what?" Fergus said with a shrug as his two favorite deerhounds came bounding into the Great Hall.

The huge dogs jumped into Fergus's lap. It was all exasperating for Queen Elinor. No one in her family seemed to know how to comport themselves in a royal manner. She turned her frustration to the triplets, who stubbornly refused to eat anything unless it was sweet.

"Boys, you're not eating your haggis!" Elinor snapped.

The triplets looked down at their bowls of gray meat and made a series of disgusted faces.

"How do you know you don't like it if you won't try it?" Elinor demanded. "It's just a wee sheep's stomach. Come on, it's delicious!"

Just then, Maudie entered the Great Hall and handed Elinor three envelopes. Elinor accepted them gratefully, happy to be distracted from her unruly family. Besides, when she saw the envelopes, her eyes widened. She was anxiously awaiting news about certain plans she was making, and these letters could be important to the future of the kingdom.

5

Elinor didn't notice the ruckus at the dinner table as she opened her letters. The dogs that had jumped into Fergus's lap were now eating off his dinner plate. "Hey, hey, hey—stay out of my food, you greedy mongrels!" Fergus said, laughing. Then he raised his wooden leg. "Chew on *that*, you manky dogs!"

Merida was secretly passing her muffins to the triplets, who refused to eat their haggis. Under the table, one of the mischievous triplets took a long napkin and tied Fergus's good leg to a table post.

Elinor looked up from her letters just as the triplets reappeared in their chairs and Merida set down her now empty plate. "Fergus?" Elinor said. "They've all accepted!"

"Who's accepted what, Mum?" Merida asked.

Elinor's face suddenly took on a serious expression. She

turned to the triplets. "Boys, you are excused."

Merida rolled her eyes. In her experience, whenever the boys were "excused," it meant she was in trouble. The triplets immediately raced away from the table. The dogs jumped up and took off after the boys, barking.

Merida shook her head. "What is it? What did I do now?"

"Your father has something to discuss with you," Elinor replied stiffly.

Fergus, suddenly surprised, spit out his drink in a wide spray. Elinor nodded at him firmly. "Fergus?" she said sternly.

Reluctantly, Fergus cleared his throat. "Merida," he began.

But Elinor couldn't contain her excitement. "The lords are presenting their sons as suitors for your betrothal!" she said with a note of triumph in her voice.

"What?" Merida said, stunned. "Betrothal?"

"The clans have accepted," Elinor said.

This was the first Merida had heard of her betrothal and marriage to anyone. She turned. "Dad?"

"What? I—uh—you . . . ," Fergus stammered. Then he pointed to Elinor and said, "She, uh—Elinor!"

Merida slumped and put her head on the table. She

didn't know exactly how this betrothal was supposed to work, but she did know she didn't want anything to do with it.

"Honestly," Elinor said, "I don't know why you're reacting this way. In the Highland Games this year, each clan will present a suitor to compete for your hand."

Merida pounded her fist on the table and shouted, "I suppose a princess just does what she's told!"

"A princess does not raise her voice!" Elinor replied. "This is what you've been preparing for your whole life."

"No," Merida said, looking at her mother. "This is what *you've* been preparing me for my whole life." Merida leaped up from the table. "I won't go through with it! You can't make me!" she said, and stormed out of the Great Hall.

"Merida!" Fergus cried, jumping to his feet to stop her. But his leg was tied to the table, and in a thundering crash, the table and Fergus were suddenly upended. The clatter of broken dishes resounded through the Great Hall. *"Boys!"* Fergus howled, knowing instantly who the culprits were.

6

Merida climbed the stone stairway that led from the Great Hall to her room and slammed the door hard. She drew her sword and vented her frustration on the curtains on her large four-poster bed, slashing them to shreds.

Then Merida held the sword with both hands, and with a swing as powerful as any Highland warrior, gave the bedpost a solid whack. She tumbled over the bed, ready to strike again, when she looked up and saw Elinor standing in the doorway.

Merida stopped in her tracks and glared at her mother. "Suitors? Marriage?" she asked.

Elinor didn't reply. Instead, she calmly crossed the room, carrying a chessboard, and sat in front of the fireplace. "Once, there was an ancient kingdom," she began.

Merida rolled her eyes and flopped onto the bed. "Oh, Mum," she said. She was suddenly exhausted by the thought of another boring lesson.

But Elinor carefully set four of the chess pieces—the knights—in a square formation on the table. She placed the king in the center and continued with her story. "Its name is long forgotten. The kingdom was ruled by a wise and fair king, who was much beloved. When the king grew old, he divided his kingdom among his four sons, that they should be the pillars on which the peace of the land rested."

Merida moved next to Elinor and watched as her mother removed the king from the center. Then she carefully balanced the chessboard filled with pieces on just the four knights. "But the oldest prince wanted to rule the land for himself. He followed his own path, and the kingdom fell to war, to chaos, and to ruin." Elinor pulled one of the knights from beneath his corner of the chessboard, causing the board to tilt and fall. All the chess pieces clattered to the floor.

"That's a nice story," Merida sighed, unimpressed.

"It's not just a story, Merida!" Elinor said, wanting desperately to get through to her daughter. "Legends are lessons. They ring with truths."

Merida turned her back and mumbled, "Och, Mum!"

Elinor drew a deep breath and said firmly, "I would advise you to make your peace with this. The clans are coming to present their suitors."

Merida began to realize she really had no choice in the matter. "It's not fair!" she protested, feeling trapped.

But her mother had lost her patience. "Merida, it's marriage! It's not the end of the world!" And with that, Elinor walked out, slamming the door behind her.

Merida didn't know how she could make her mother understand that the loss of her freedom seemed much worse than the end of the world.

7

Above the Great Hall and just beyond the family's bedchambers was the castle's Tapestry Room. On one wall hung a large tapestry showing Clan DunBroch in happier times. Fergus, in his finest kilt, was shown standing proudly behind his family. Elinor stood nearby, and stitched into the design close to both of them was their adoring young daughter, Merida. The triplets were well groomed, and at least appeared to be well behaved.

Elinor entered the room and picked up her embroidery, glancing at the tapestry. She wished life could be as manageable as what could be stitched into a tapestry.

Just then, Fergus poked his head into the room. "You're muttering," he told his wife.

"I don't mutter," Elinor replied, refusing to look up.

"Aye, you do," he said with a chuckle. "You mutter, lass, when something's troubling you."

Elinor kept her eyes on her embroidery. "I blame you!" she said. "It's entirely from your side of the family."

Fergus smiled and entered the room. He had to admit that Merida did get her taste for adventure from his side, as surely as she'd inherited his fiery red hair. "I take it the talk didn't go too well, then?" Fergus asked.

Elinor sighed and stopped stitching. She looked up at Fergus. "I don't know what to do."

"Speak to her, dear," Fergus replied.

"I do speak to her; she just doesn't listen," Elinor said.

Fergus grabbed a stool and sat next to Elinor. "Come on, now," he said, hoping to raise her spirits. "Pretend I'm Merida. Speak to me. What would you say?"

Elinor furrowed her brow. "Och. I can't do this."

"Sure you can," Fergus said kindly.

Elinor looked into his big, open face and regained her queenly composure.

"That's my queen," Fergus said. He tried to imitate Merida's voice, hoping to get Elinor started. "I don't want to get married," he said in a high voice. "I want to stay single and let my hair flow in the wind as I ride through the glen firing arrows into the sunset!"

"Merida," Elinor said, looking into Fergus's eyes. "All this work, all the time we've spent preparing you, schooling you, giving you everything we never had. I ask you, what do you expect us to do? I understand that this all must seem unfair. Even I had reservations when I faced betrothal."

"Huh?" Fergus said, surprised.

"But we can't run away from who we are," Elinor continued. "If you could just try to see that what I do, I do out of love." She paused and said finally, "I think you'd see that if you'd just . . . listen."

At that very same moment, Merida was in Angus's stall. She was placing fresh straw on the floor, but mostly she was just speaking to Angus, trying to clear her mind.

Merida knew her mother had the power to make all this betrothal nonsense stop. She looked at Angus and tried to pretend she was speaking to Elinor.

"Call off the gathering—would that kill them? You're the queen. You could tell the lords, 'The princess is not ready for this. In fact, she might never be ready for this, so that's that. G'day to you! We'll expect your declarations of war in the morning.'"

Angus tilted his head, trying to understand. Merida

looked into his big brown eyes. "I don't want my life to be over. I want my freedom. I think I could make you understand if you'd just . . . listen," she said, envisioning her mother's face.

Angus snorted and bobbed his head, snapping Merida out of the moment. Merida sighed and said firmly, "I swear, Angus, this isn't going to happen. Not if I have any say in it."

But not many days later, Merida woke to the sound of drums coming from the longships as they sailed into DunBroch Harbor.

Her suitors had arrived.

8

Lord Macintosh, wearing a blue kilt and a tartan sash, stood proudly at the bow of his wooden longship. The blue-painted faces of his clan chanted, "Mac-in-tosh!" as the ship's beating drum helped drive the oarsmen steadily into DunBroch Harbor.

Lord Macintosh was taken aback when Lord MacGuffin's boat suddenly pulled up alongside. Young MacGuffin, one of Merida's hopeful suitors, began chanting to the beat of his own ship's drum: "Mac-Guff-in! Mac-Guff-in!" Soon his entire clan joined in, shouting, "Mac-Guff-in!"

Then those two ships were joined by a third, belonging to the Dingwall clan. Old Lord Dingwall began the chant and was soon joined by Wee Dingwall and the rest of his clan in shouting, "Ding-wall! Ding-wall! Ding-wall!"

As the clans rowed harder and chanted louder, one drummer broke his drumsticks to splinters. But he carried on with the two jagged stumps. This was a competition no clan wanted to lose. Everyone knew that arriving first would make a good impression, and could influence the royal family. Each of the lords was determined to have his own son win Princess Merida's hand . . . and rise to the rank of prince. And each dreamed of a future heir who might someday be king.

Inside Castle DunBroch, Merida watched from her window as the lords sailed into the sparkling harbor. She turned away in anger. Her fate and freedom were in someone else's hands now. She was just a playing piece on the chessboard, and everyone seemed to be enjoying the game but her.

Merida held her breath as Queen Elinor strapped her into a tight corset. Then Elinor pulled a long blue velvet gown over her daughter's head. She brushed Merida's wildly curly hair and neatly stuffed it into an elegant, snug-fitting hood called a wimple. Merida looked at herself in the mirror. She felt like a goose—stuffed, trussed, and ready for the roaster.

Elinor, already wearing a long, flowing green gown, gasped. "You look absolutely beautiful!"

"I . . . I can't breathe!" Merida croaked.

"Och!" Elinor said, and waved the complaint away. "Give us a turn."

Merida waddled around in a circle. "I can't move," she moaned. "It's too tight."

But Elinor was delighted. "It's perfect!"

Merida looked pleadingly into her mother's eyes. Suddenly, Elinor paused. She seemed to want to say something more to Merida. Then Elinor dropped her gaze and the moment passed. "Just remember to smile" was all she said.

9

The castle guards peeked through the doors of the Great Hall and watched the lords march in, flanked by their burly clans. "Och! They're coming!" one of the guards shouted.

Inside the Great Hall, the royal family stood on a low platform, ready to receive the visitors. "Places, everyone, places!" Elinor said, motioning to Merida to be seated on her throne. Merida took her place but defiantly pulled a curl from her wimple and let it fall between her eyes. Elinor immediately tucked it back in.

Then Elinor turned to Fergus, who was handsomely dressed. She began to adjust his red plaid kilt and sash. "I look fine, woman. Let me be," he protested. But Elinor kept fussing with him nervously. "Let me be, I tell you!"

Fergus said as he batted her hand away. Behind him, Merida pulled out her curl again.

From the back of the Great Hall, the guard called out in a loud, clear voice, "My lord, I announce the arrival of Lord Dingwall!" But before he could announce the names of any other lords, the surly clans kicked the Great Hall's door and it flew open, pinning him against the wall.

The sound of bagpipes suddenly filled the hall as all three lords—Macintosh, MacGuffin, and Dingwall—gruffly entered the room, along with their attendants.

As they approached the queen's and king's thrones on the dais, Lord Dingwall, who was shorter than the other lords, yelled, "Boy!" A skinny lad suddenly came running with a footstool. When Lord Dingwall stepped up onto the stool, raising his height to match the other lords', his clan began shouting their war cries. The other clans joined in until Fergus, regal and mighty, stood up. The room suddenly went quiet.

Fergus cleared his throat. "I—uh—" he began, stammering as he addressed the clans. As usual, during events that required him to speak, he suddenly became unsure of what to say. "So, uh . . . here we are, the, uh . . . clans."

Elinor cringed and put her head in her hands. Merida was even more distressed. She was hunched over on her throne, frantically trying to think up a plan. "How do I get out of this?" she kept asking herself over and over as Fergus stumbled through his awkward greeting.

"And . . . now y-you're here. And we're all together," Fergus said. He kept nodding and struggling for his next word until Elinor couldn't stand another minute of his mumbling. She quickly stood up and, with a wave of her arm, took over.

"We have gathered for the presentation of the suitors," she said smoothly.

Fergus smiled, happy to be rescued, and repeated enthusiastically, "Aye! The presentation of the suitors!" The crowd cheered and Merida rolled her eyes.

"Clan Macintosh!" Fergus called, and wiry Lord Macintosh stepped forward. The Macintosh clan whooped as Lord Macintosh said grandly, "Your Majesty, I present my heir, the scion who defended our land from the Northern Invaders, and, with his own sword, Stab Blooder, vanquished a thousand foes!"

Young Macintosh, whipping his long hair out of his eyes, walked to the front of the dais, swinging his sword. Merida took one look at the tall and arrogant Young Macintosh and pulled her wimple over her eyes.

Next, Fergus called, "Clan MacGuffin!"

The chanting turned to "MacGuffin! MacGuffin!" as the thick-chested Lord MacGuffin came forward. "Good Majesty," MacGuffin began, "I present my eldest son, who scuttled the Vikings' longships, and with his bare hands vanquished two thousand foes!"

Merida peeked out from under her wimple to see beefy Young MacGuffin carrying a giant log in his hands. The rowdy clan cheered as the young warrior easily snapped the log in two.

Then Fergus called out, "Clan Dingwall!" Old Lord Dingwall stepped down from his footstool and stood beside a massive, muscled warrior who was far larger than the other suitors. Elinor and Fergus were impressed. Merida was horrified.

"I present my only son, who was besieged by ten thousand Romans. And he took out a whole armada single-handedly!" The brute was so huge, Merida could almost believe it.

Dingwall continued proudly, "With one arm, he was . . ." Dingwall hesitated for a moment, staring at the giant soldier . . . then reached behind the muscle-bound warrior and pulled his son into view. Merida, Fergus, and Elinor were stunned to see the scrawny, short, and weak-chinned Wee Dingwall.

A voice called out, "Lies!"

"What? I heard that!" Lord Dingwall yelled as he jumped up and down, trying to see who in the crowd had made the accusation. It didn't take much to get the clans warring, and an insult like that would never be borne. "Go on! Say it to my face! Or are you scared? Simpering jackanapes, afraid to muss your pretty hair?" Lord Dingwall huffed, nodding at Young Macintosh.

"At least we *have* hair!" Lord Macintosh replied with a laugh.

"And all our teeth," Lord MacGuffin said, chuckling. "And we don't hide under bridges, you grumpy old troll!"

The crowd howled. Even Fergus joined in. Wee Dingwall was fuming. But Lord Dingwall just crossed his arms over his chest. "You want to laugh, eh?" he said smugly. "Wee Dingwall!"

Suddenly, Wee Dingwall's face transformed into a ferocious mask. He dove at Lord Macintosh, growling and biting his neck. Everyone, including Merida, was shocked.

Old Lord Dingwall cackled with glee . . . until Young Macintosh turned and punched the old lord right in the face. That was it. The fuse was lit. The Great Hall suddenly exploded into a wild Highland brawl!

IO

The bagpipes kept playing as the clans lunged at each other, grunting and howling and knocking one another to the floor. Wee Dingwall hit the ground but just as quickly leaped up and bit the leg of a nearby warrior.

Up on the dais, Fergus was enjoying the brawl immensely, cheering all sides on, until Elinor gave him a stern look. Fergus heaved a sigh, then reluctantly stood up and yelled, "SHUT IT!"

The fighting came to an immediate halt and the bagpipes sadly droned to a stop. "You've had your go at each other!" Fergus shouted. "Now show a little decorum—no more fighting!"

Unseen, the triplets popped through a trapdoor in the floor and hit Lord Dingwall's foot with a club. As Dingwall howled in pain, a giant fist came out of the crowd and punched his face. Suddenly, the bagpipes started up and the brawl was in full swing again!

Wee Dingwall was riding on the shoulders of a fellow clan member. His mouth was open, ready to bite, as he punched his way through the crowd.

Young MacGuffin grabbed a long bench and began swinging it in a wide arc, knocking six men to the ground. The bagpipers ducked when the bench whizzed past their heads.

Fergus was enjoying the fight so much, he couldn't help throwing himself into the swarm of brawling Highlanders. He dove from the dais and sent a warrior reeling. He lifted another and tossed him through the air. The man landed near the triplets, who promptly hit him with a club and knocked him out.

Elinor had seen enough. She stood up, straightened her dress, and calmly walked into the midst of the ruckus. The brawling crowd suddenly parted, revealing Fergus and the lords in a tangle, still hitting each other.

"You want a fresh one?" Fergus roared, raising his fist. Then he and the lords suddenly saw Elinor. The fighting men froze.

Elinor took Fergus and the lords by the ear like

schoolboys and dragged them out of the crowd. "*Ow! Ow! Ow!*" they screamed, until she released them. Elinor brushed off her hands and returned to the dais.

"Sorry," Lord Dingwall said sheepishly to Queen Elinor.

"I didn't start it," Lord Macintosh said quickly. "M'lady, my humblest apologies."

"So sorry, Your Highness," Lord MacGuffin added. "We meant no disrespect!"

Fergus looked down and mumbled, "Sorry, luv, I didn't—"

Elinor stopped Fergus with a wave of her hand and directed him to take his seat. Head bowed, Fergus obeyed, saying, "Yes, dear." Then he silently signaled to Dingwall that he'd get him later.

Elinor ignored him and addressed the crowd. "Now, where were we? Ah, yes . . . In accordance with our laws, by the rights of our heritage, only the firstborn of each of the great leaders may be presented as champion and thus compete for the hand of the princess of DunBroch."

Merida sat up straight. "Firstborn?" she repeated to herself, an idea suddenly occurring to her. She listened carefully as Elinor continued.

"To win the fair maiden, they must prove their worth by feats of strength or arms in the Games. It is customary that the challenge be determined by the princess herself."

Merida jumped to her feet, barely able to contain herself. "Archery! Archery!" she yelled. She caught a sharp glance from her mother and quickly regained her composure. Merida demurely clasped her hands and carefully pronounced, "I choose archery."

Elinor smiled approvingly, turned to the crowd, and said, "Then let the Games begin!"

11

Banners streamed in the wind and colorful tents dotted the castle green, giving it a festive air. The crowd cheered as the visiting clans competed in a multitude of traditional games. A raised platform stood at one end of the field so the royal family could view the day's competition clearly. Merida, Fergus, and Elinor watched warriors tossing weights over a high beam, which was gradually raised higher and higher.

Elsewhere, two groups played an aggressive game of cricket. Suddenly, the ball flew across the green and whacked Wee Dingwall in the head. But Young MacGuffin and Young Macintosh didn't notice their rival fall. They were busy competing in a throwing event, each one tossing a huge rock as far as possible. Young MacGuffin out-tossed Young Macintosh, who immediately stomped on the ground and started crying.

The rowdy crowd booed and cheered in turns. They were having an all-around fine time! Highland dancers performed as the bagpipes played. There were tents of food, and good smells filled the air.

Meanwhile, the triplets were scurrying happily through the crowd when they spotted Maudie carrying a tray of sweets. They immediately hatched a plan. Climbing to the top of a tent, two of the triplets lowered the third down toward Maudie's tray.

Maudie turned and saw the dangling boy. "Oh!" she cried angrily. Caught, the triplets on the tent dropped their brother and slipped away. Maudie grabbed the remaining one and immediately scolded him. "Now, I've told you, you're not allowed!"

While Maudie was distracted, the two other boys snatched the tray from behind her and ran off. *Success!*

Minutes later, all three boys met behind the tent and ate the entire tray of sweets, as planned. And as often happened with Maudie, she was left scratching her head, wondering what had just gone on.

Suddenly, everyone heard the carynx, the ancient Celtic

horn used for calling the clans together. Even the dogs howled at the sound. The main competition was about to begin!

Fergus stepped to the front of the stage. "It's time!" he announced to the excited crowd. "Well, you didn't come all this way for nothing, now, did ya?" He smiled and looked around blankly. "Uh, so, uh . . ."

Elinor stood and called out, "Archers, to your marks!"

"Aye!" Fergus repeated. "Archers, to your marks!"

The crowd cheered as the suitors stood before their clan banners. "And may the lucky arrow find its target!" Elinor proclaimed. Merida smiled and looked at her bow, which she had secretly tucked away on the side of the platform.

12

Merida looked at the young lords as they stepped forward. She leaned toward Fergus, who was seated on his throne. "Dad, you think any of these gormless neeps can hit anything?"

Fergus chuckled. Young MacGuffin stood confidently, holding his bow, while Young Macintosh strutted arrogantly and pointed to the target. Wee Dingwall didn't seem to know what the bow was for. He held it like a harp and dumbly plucked at the string.

"Oi! Get on with it!" Fergus shouted at them.

Young MacGuffin was ready to take the first shot. The crowd held its breath as he loosed his arrow.

"Och!" Lord MacGuffin yelled in disappointment as Young MacGuffin's arrow missed the target completely.

Merida leaned toward Fergus. "What a numpty," she said with a giggle. "I bet he wishes he was tossing cabers!"

"Or holding up bridges!" Fergus said, laughing. Elinor heard them and shushed them both.

Vain Young Macintosh came next. He gave his long hair a proud toss and shot his arrow. He hit the target, but his aim was off center. The crowd was stunned when Macintosh stomped about and wailed, unhappy at having missed the bull's-eye.

"At least you hit the target, son!" Lord Macintosh called out. But Young Macintosh didn't care. He raised his bow above his head and beat it on the ground.

"Oh, that's attractive," Merida commented, watching as Young Macintosh angrily threw his bow into the crowd.

"And such lovely, flowing locks," Fergus said with a snicker.

"Fergus!" Elinor snapped.

"What?" Fergus said innocently.

Finally, it was Wee Dingwall's turn. As he approached the target, he spilled most of his arrows onto the ground. He drew one of the remaining arrows from his quiver and fumbled with his bow. "Oh, wee lamb," Merida sighed.

"Oh, come on! Shoot, boy!" Fergus yelled.

Startled, Wee Dingwall accidentally let loose an

arrow and—*Thump!* Bull's-eye! The crowd roared! Wee Dingwall looked at the target in shock and delight.

"Well done, lad! That's my boy!" Lord Dingwall cried out, doing a jig. Then Lord Dingwall danced over to Lord Macintosh and Lord MacGuffin. He turned his back to them, leaned over, then raised his kilt and yelled, "Feast your eyes!" The rival lords gritted their teeth as old Dingwall gloated.

Fergus looked up at the sky. "Well, that's just grand, now, isn't it?" he said with a sigh, thinking of how it would be with the Dingwall clan as his in-laws. "Guess who's coming to dinner!"

Fergus leaned toward Merida's throne. "Oh, by the way, hope you like being called Lady Dingwall." But Merida was gone. One of the family deerhounds was sitting in her place.

The crowd's attention was suddenly caught by a small hooded figure walking to the center of the field. A gasp rose from the audience as the figure ripped off the hooded cloak and thrust a pole bearing the DunBroch colors into the ground. It was Merida. And her bow was in her hand.

"I am Merida, firstborn descendant of Clan DunBroch!" she called out fiercely, standing tall and proud. "And I'll be shooting for my own hand!"

Elinor was shocked. "What are you doing?" she called to her daughter.

But Merida didn't flinch. She placed her arrow in her bow, but her dress was too tight for her to shoot. "Curse this dress," Merida muttered as she took a deep breath and drew back on the bow with all her might. The seams of her dress ripped. The crowd was stunned into silence as Merida aimed her bow at Young MacGuffin's target. *Thwap!* She hit it dead center.

"Merida, stop this!" Elinor demanded. But Merida ignored her mother. She moved on to Young Macintosh's target and easily hit that bull's-eye, too.

Elinor charged off the royal dais, angrily calling for Merida to stop. But she could barely be heard over Young Macintosh's wailing.

Wee Dingwall's target was next. By some miracle, he had hit a bull's-eye. Merida knew there was only one thing she could do. She aimed her bow and . . . *WHAP!* She split his arrow with her own. Merida folded her arms across her chest and smiled.

13

Elinor dragged Merida up the stone stairs that led from the Great Hall to the Tapestry Room. She slammed the door behind her so none of their guests would hear how angry she was. "Mighty me!" Elinor said, fuming. "I've had just about enough of you, lass!"

"You're the one—" Merida began, but there would be no arguing with her mother today.

"You embarrassed them! You embarrassed me! You don't know what you've done!" Elinor said, pacing around the room. "It will be fire and sword if it's not set right."

"Just listen!" Merida pleaded.

But Elinor was too angry. "I am the QUEEN! You listen to *me*!" she yelled.

"Arrrgh! This is so unfair," Merida said, turning away

from her mother and fiddling with a sword in a rack.

"Unfair?" Elinor asked her.

"This whole marriage is what *you* want!" Merida responded. "Do you ever bother to ask me what *I* want? *Nooooo*. You walk around telling me what to do, what not to do, trying to make me be like you. Well, I'm not going to be like you!"

"Och!" Elinor replied, dismissing her daughter's talk as nonsense. "You're acting like a child."

It was Merida who spoke in anger now. "And you're a beast! That's what you are!" Merida moved toward the family tapestry with the sword in her hand. "I'll never be like you!" she said, poking the tapestry with the sword's point.

"Merida!" Elinor warned. "Stop that!"

"I'd rather *die* than be like you!" Merida exclaimed. In a fit of anger, she slashed at the family tapestry, ripping a long gash between the images of herself and her mother.

Elinor was horrified. She marched toward Merida, took the sword from her hand, and tossed it away. "Merida," she said through clenched teeth. "You are a princess, and I expect you to act like one." Then Elinor grabbed Merida's prized bow—the one Merida had received from Fergus as a wee child—and threw it into the fireplace.

Merida gasped. In a blur of tears and anger, she flung open the door and ran. She had to get away from the castle.

In the Tapestry Room, Elinor breathed heavily, furious. Then she paused—and saw Merida's bow in the fireplace. Her anger turned to horror, and she quickly fished the bow out of the embers. She knew the bow was important to Merida and hadn't meant to harm it.

But Merida didn't see that. She was already at the stables, swinging up onto Angus's back. Together they raced out the castle gates.

Angus galloped through the rugged woods at full speed. Brush and twigs caught in Merida's hair as Angus rode farther from home than either of them had ever gone before.

Suddenly, Angus reared up, throwing Merida to the ground. Merida stood, wiped the dirt and tears from her eyes, and realized she had landed at the edge of a large circle of stones. Angus stayed outside the circle and whinnied uneasily.

A heavy gray mist had settled over the land, but Merida was able to make out a glowing blue light flickering between the stones. She closed her eyes, thinking she was imagining it. But when she opened them, the tiny blue light was still there, glowing in the mist. It seemed to be beckoning her, calling to her in a soft and steady whisper.

Merida walked toward the tiny blue light. Slowly, she reached out her hand to touch it and the light disappeared. Merida turned to Angus, who was still cowering at the edge of the circle. "Come on, Angus," she called to him. The horse hesitated. The circle seemed to make him nervous. "Angus!" Merida called again.

Angus pulled back, hiding behind one of the large stones as Merida turned and saw the light again. She followed the light as it led her outside the circle. Angus ran around the circle to meet her on the other side. When he reached Merida, he nuzzled against her and they followed the blue light together.

Suddenly, the single blue light was joined by a line of tiny lights. Together they created a path for Merida and Angus to follow through a dark forest of withered trees covered in hanging moss, and up the crest of a hill. Finally, the blue lights led them to a small thatched cottage. A wood-hewn sign hung over the door: **THE CRAFTY CARVER**. At the door, the lights scattered back into the mist.

Curious, Merida peeked through the cottage's dark window. Seeing nothing, she knocked on the door.

An old, bony woman dusted with wood shavings slowly opened the door. She had one eye that bulged out terribly, but otherwise, she seemed normal enough. She bid Merida to enter, and in the cottage's dim light, Merida could see wood carvings of bears everywhere.

"Would you care to buy one?" the old woman asked, holding up one carving after another.

Merida was not especially interested in wood carvings, but there was something odd about the place that intrigued her. For one thing, there was a crow that seemed to have been stuffed and placed on the head of a bear carving, but every now and then the bird blinked. Then Merida noticed a broom in the corner, sweeping a bit of dust by itself. Merida was no fool. The old woman was a witch . . . and witches could be quite useful when a person had a problem with no solution.

Merida decided to be bold. "If I could just change my mum, my life would be better," she declared. "Can you give me a spell?"

The old woman glared at Merida and shooed her toward the door. "If you're not going to buy anything, you should leave!" she shouted.

Desperate, Merida tried one last time. "What if I buy all your carvings?" she said. "If you give me *one* spell, I'll buy everything here!"

The old woman stopped and stared. Then she nodded.

She pushed Merida outside the cottage. They both stood there for a moment. Then the old woman led Merida back in and slammed the door. Everything had changed! All the carvings were suddenly gone. The crow fluttered down from the rafters and landed on the Witch's shoulder, and the broom scurried freely around the room. A large cauldron sat in the center of the room. The Witch spit and said, "Now, what kind of spell do you want, lass?"

14

"What kind of spell can you do?" Merida asked eagerly.

"Ooh! I've done them all!" the Witch said as she began tossing things into a bag. Merida anxiously followed her around the cottage. "Make you taller, shorter, smarter, stronger? Make someone fall in love with you, make you fly, make your castle fly?"

"Talk to animals?" the crow asked.

"Not my favorite," the Witch remarked bitterly as she went on. "Breathe underwater? How about a unicorn? Would you like one of those?"

"It's my mother," Merida explained. "She lives to ruin my life. Always this and never do that, and wake up, dear, time to marry some dafty lord's ham-fisted son! If my mum were different, if I could change her . . ."

The Witch suddenly had a faraway look on her wrinkled face. "Long ago, I met a prince. A willful lad he was."

"Easy on the eyes," the crow squawked.

The Witch shot him a nasty look and held out her bony hand to Merida. "He gave me this ring," she said. Merida looked at the gold ring with two crossed axes. "He demanded I give him the strength of ten men. A spell that would change his life."

"And did he get what he was after?" Merida asked.

"Aye," the Witch replied.

Merida was suddenly filled with hope. "Then that's what I want!" she cried. "I want a spell that changes my mother. That will change my fate."

"Done," the Witch proclaimed, and quickly began tossing things into her cauldron.

15

Merida watched, intrigued, as the old woman scurried around the cottage, gathering dried herbs and pieces of rotted bark. "Now I'll need just a little bit of this, and . . . ah!" the Witch mumbled excitedly. She sniffed something between her fingers and dropped it into the cauldron.

Angus stood at the window, nervously watching the woman as she ran back and forth. She tossed something slimy into the cauldron and smiled. "Yes, in you go," she said, satisfied. "Lovely!" Then she took a newt from a jar and threw that in as well. The brew in the cauldron slowly began to bubble.

The crow plucked a hair from Merida's head and dropped it into the pot. "And a little of this," the Witch mumbled, adding a pinch of powdered root. "Yes! That'll do."

The Witch stepped up onto a stool and stirred the pot with a large spoon. When she pulled it out, Merida was surprised to see that most of the spoon had disintegrated. But the Witch merely tossed it aside.

She sprinkled in a few more ingredients, then placed a protective mask over the crow's face and one over her own. The Witch covered Merida's face with her hand, and—*BOOM!* The concoction suddenly exploded, sending a flash of light bursting from the windows and the chimney.

Merida's face was covered in soot except for the outline of the Witch's hand. As she sputtered and coughed, she saw that the cauldron was glowing a bright green.

The Witch leaned over it and said, "Oh! Now, let's see. What do we have here?" Using tongs, she reached in and pulled a perfect, dainty little cake from the steaming cauldron.

She quickly swept the clutter off a table and set the cake on a cloth. The crow began to peck at it. "A cake?" Merida asked, surprised and disappointed.

The Witch slapped the bird away. "You remember what happened last time?" she said to the crow.

"A man!" the crow squawked. "I was a man!"

"Dumb bird," the Witch grumbled. Then she pointed at the cake. "You don't want it?" she asked Merida.

"Yes, I want it!" Merida said quickly. Then she added, to confirm, "So if I give this to my mum, it will change my fate, right?"

The Witch nodded.

Carrying the cake, Merida stepped outside. Still puzzled by how the spell was supposed to work, she hesitated and turned back to the cottage.

But the cottage was gone. Whirling back in the other direction, Merida saw the Ring of Stones. They were much closer to Merida and Angus than before. Merida blinked, and she and Angus were suddenly standing alone in the mist, again surrounded by the huge stones.

16

Angus and Merida hurried back to Castle DunBroch. She settled Angus into his stall and quietly entered the castle through the kitchen door. She peeked into the room first to make sure no one was about. When she was sure the coast was clear, she unwrapped the tiny cake. She wanted to make it look as delicious as possible, so she set it on a tray with a pot of tea and a fresh-cut flower.

"Merida?" Elinor said as she entered the kitchen. Merida nearly jumped out of her skin. "Where have you been? I've been worried sick!"

Merida gulped. "You were?"

"Of course," her mother replied. "I didn't know where you had gone. I didn't know what to think!"

"Uh, Angus threw me, but I'm not hurt," Merida said,

making something up quickly to explain her disheveled state.

Elinor smiled and said, "Well, you're home now, so that's the end of it."

"Oh, honestly?" Merida asked hopefully. She wondered if the betrothal plans had changed.

"Of course. I've pacified the lords for now," Elinor said, and Merida's hopeful expression disappeared. Elinor motioned to the Great Hall. "Your father's out there 'entertaining' them."

In the Great Hall, Fergus was up on the dais. He was singing "The Ballad of Mor'du" to the rough crowd.

"*Come taste my blade, you manky bear, for gobbling up my leg,*" Fergus sang, dancing on his wooden leg as he waved his sword. "*I'll hunt you, then I'll skin you, hang your noggin on a peg!*"

The crowd roared its approval—all except the lords, who were still grumpy about the rejection of their sons. They sat there, stone-faced, as Fergus and the crowd heartily sang the old bear's name. "*Mor'du, Mor'du, Mor'du!*"

From inside the kitchen, Elinor and Merida could hear the singing. "Of course, you know a decision still has to be made," Elinor said. Merida frowned. She felt she had no choice now. She brought the tray with the cake on it to her

Princess Merida has a free and adventurous spirit.
After a full day of roaming in the forest, she goes
home to dinner with lots of stories—and a big appetite.

Merida lives with her family in Castle DunBroch.
The castle sits atop a mountain in the ancient wilds
of Scotland, a land of mist and magic.

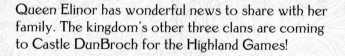

Queen Elinor has wonderful news to share with her family. The kingdom's other three clans are coming to Castle DunBroch for the Highland Games!

King Fergus and Queen Elinor explain that this year's Games will carry special importance. Merida is not thrilled with the news.

The clan lords' firstborn sons will compete for Merida's hand in marriage. But Merida isn't ready to marry anyone!

Even though Wee Dingwall can barely hold a bow, he manages to hit the bull's-eye during the archery contest.

Merida steps forward and announces that she will compete for her own hand!

The lords are shocked to see Merida taking aim—and defying the clans' traditions.

Merida hits three bull's-eyes in a row and wins the competition!

Queen Elinor is not pleased. She worries that Merida's actions will lead to feuding among the clans.

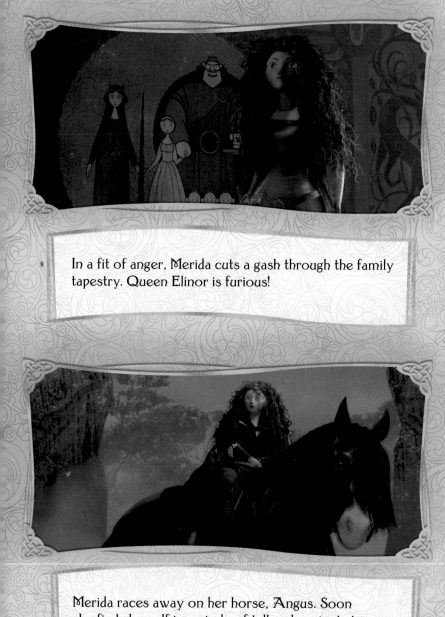

In a fit of anger, Merida cuts a gash through the family tapestry. Queen Elinor is furious!

Merida races away on her horse, Angus. Soon she finds herself in a circle of tall and ancient stones.

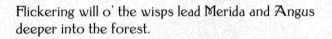

Flickering will o' the wisps lead Merida and Angus deeper into the forest.

Bears appear often in the legends of Clan DunBroch, but this bear is unlike any other.

To protect his daughter from the bear, King Fergus locks her in the Tapestry Room.

Luckily, three bear cubs arrive to help Merida escape from the locked room so she can set things right in the kingdom.

mother. Elinor looked down at the dainty cake in surprise.

"It's a peace offering," Merida said. "I made it for you! Special!"

"You made this for me?" Elinor asked, and placed a piece of the cake in her mouth. She found it a bit hard to swallow but gracefully smiled and wiped the corners of her mouth.

Merida's eyes widened. "How do you feel, Mum? Different?"

"Hmm, interesting flavor," Elinor replied. "What is that? It's tart and gamey." She took a sip of tea to help her swallow the cake more easily.

Merida kept staring into her mother's face. "Have you changed your mind about the marriage and all?"

All Merida's hopes began to fade as her mother gave her a pat on the hand and escorted her toward the Great Hall. "Now, why don't we go upstairs to the lords and put this whole kerfuffle to rest, hmm?" Elinor said.

Merida's heart sank. "Nothing happened," she mumbled to herself.

They were nearing the Great Hall when Elinor stumbled. Merida caught her by the elbow. "I'm woozy suddenly," Elinor said. "My head is spinning like a top! Oh! I'm not well at all."

Merida thought the cake might be working. "How do

you feel about the marriage now?" she asked anxiously.

But all Elinor could do was moan and say, "Merida, just take me to my room." Merida took her mother's arm and steered her toward the stairs. She felt sorry that Elinor was sick, but was relieved to be able to avoid the clans a bit longer.

17

In the Great Hall, the clan warriors moved one of Fergus's stuffed trophy bears to the middle of the room. "A little to the left!" Fergus instructed, raising an axe and aiming it at the bear's head. "That's good! Now clear out of there, boys. I don't want you to spoil my shot."

The lords noticed Merida and Elinor heading for the staircase that led to the bedchambers upstairs. The lords quickly intercepted them. "M'lady," Lord MacGuffin said. "We've been waiting patiently."

"Aye," Lord Macintosh added. "With assurances from you of a decision upon the princess's return."

Lord Dingwall pointed to Merida. "And there she be!"

Merida felt trapped. Her fate could be decided at any moment.

But Elinor was too ill to make any decision. "My lords, I am out of sorts at the moment. But you'll have your answer presently. Now, if you'll excuse us." Elinor suddenly made a sound from deep in her stomach, and the lords stepped back. Merida helped her up the stone staircase.

Fergus noticed them and shouted, "Elinor, look! It's Mor'du!"

"Dad, it's a stuffed bear," Merida said.

Then Fergus saw Elinor's pale face and lowered his axe. "Are you all right, Elinor?"

"Fine," Elinor said with a feeble wave. "I'm fine. Go back to avenging your leg."

Fergus shrugged and turned his attention back to the crowd. "Aye, you heard her, lads!" he shouted, and broke into song again. Then Fergus hurled his axe and struck the stuffed bear right between the eyes.

From upstairs, Merida could hear the crowd cheering. She opened the door to Elinor's room and struggled to move her mother into bed. "Just take all the time you need getting yourself right, Mum. Then maybe in a bit, you might have something new to say about the marriage!"

"What was in that cake?" Elinor asked feverishly as she wrapped herself in the bed covers and moaned. Then she suddenly rolled off the edge of the big bed.

"Mum?" Merida asked. "So I'll tell them the wedding's off, then?"

Elinor's hand reached up and grabbed the bedpost. She pulled herself to stand, then slipped back to the floor. "Mum!" Merida cried, slowly moving to where her mother was lying. The white sheets Elinor was wrapped in began to rise like a ghost. Merida stared at the form under the sheets, which grew higher and higher. Then the sheets dropped away and Merida found herself gaping at a huge bear.

"*AAAAHHHHH!*" Merida screamed as the creature walked toward her. "*B-B-BEAR!*"

The creature turned and saw the shadow of a bear on the wall—and screamed as well! It dove to the floor and seemed to want to say, "There's a bear in the castle!" But only a growl came from its mouth.

Startled and confused, Elinor-Bear pointed to her throat . . . and realized that her hands were *bear claws*! Terrified, she grabbed a mirror from the dresser. She roared in shock when she saw her reflection. She quickly stood up. Her head hit the ceiling and she tripped over the bed, smashing the dresser.

As Merida watched, she slowly realized it wasn't just

some bear thrashing around the room in a panic. "Mum?" she said softly. She continued, dumbfounded. "You're a bear?" Merida stamped her foot. "Why a bear?" she asked herself angrily. "That scaffy old Witch gave me a gammy spell!"

Merida saw her mother's expression sharpen, as if she'd asked, "A witch?"

"It's not my fault!" Merida protested. "I didn't ask her to change you into a bear. I just wanted her to change ... you." Merida put her hands over her head as she realized what the Witch had done.

Elinor understood as well, and let out a roar that could be heard throughout the castle.

18

Downstairs in the Great Hall, Fergus was still throwing weapons at the stuffed bear when he suddenly stopped. "Did you hear that?" he asked. He sniffed the air. Everyone stopped their bellowing.

Lord MacGuffin swallowed a mouthful of food and asked, "What is it?"

"Something's not right," Fergus said, sniffing again. He moved toward the staircase. Then he drew his sword and bellowed, "Everybody, follow me—and keep a sharp eye!"

The clans followed Fergus up the stairs. But the old lords lagged behind. "Here we go," Lord Dingwall sighed. "Another 'hunt' through the castle."

"Aye, and we haven't even had dessert yet," Lord MacGuffin complained.

Upstairs, Elinor-Bear was still grumbling at Merida, giving her an earful of growls. "There's no point in having a go at me," Merida said. "The Witch is to blame. Googly old hag."

But that didn't satisfy Elinor-Bear. She reached down angrily, found her crown next to the bed, and put it on. Then she tried to find something to wear. Everything was much too small for her now, so she wrapped herself in a sheet and stormed out into the hallway.

"Wait!" Merida called out. "What are you doing? You can't go out there! Remember dad, the Bear King? If he sees you, you're dead for sure!"

Merida followed her mother. She could hear Fergus and the mob from the Great Hall getting closer. Merida gasped. Fergus and all the clans were suddenly in sight, but they turned a corner without seeing Merida and her mother.

With his nostrils flared, Fergus took another deep breath. Catching the scent again, he turned around. Lord Dingwall sighed as they followed along. The lords were growing weary of all the sneaking down hallways. "Best to humor him," Dingwall said. "He is, after all, the king."

Fergus was getting closer and closer to Merida and Elinor. Then Elinor-Bear turned a corner and her huge body knocked over a candleholder. Fergus heard the crash and drew his sword. One of his eyes twitched, and he smiled as he whispered, "Follow me."

Merida was trailing behind Elinor-Bear, who was still walking about as if nothing had changed. Finally, Merida yanked Elinor's sheet off and whispered, "Stop! Stop!"

Elinor-Bear, wearing only a crown, quickly tried to cover her body with her paws. Merida rolled her eyes. "You're covered with fur, Mum, you're not naked. It's not like anyone's going to see you."

They both suddenly turned at the sound of someone coming. It was Maudie. Elinor began to roar, wanting to explain to the nursemaid what had happened. But poor Maudie screamed at the sight of a bear. She turned and bolted down the hall.

"Now you've done it," Merida moaned.

Maudie kept screaming until she ran headlong into Fergus with his drawn sword. "Maudie?" Fergus asked, but she was too shaken to answer. "Just calm down, lass. What is it?"

"B-b-b-b-b-b—" Maudie said, stuttering in terror.

"Spit it out, Maudie!" Fergus yelled.

Finally, Maudie screamed, "*A BEAR!*"

"I knew it!" Fergus shouted triumphantly. He pushed Maudie aside and charged down the hall.

Merida and Elinor heard the clamoring of Fergus and his men running toward them. "Quick, this way!" Merida called to her mother, but in their panic, each ran in a different direction.

Elinor-Bear ran into a dead end in one of the castle hallways. Trapped, she ducked behind a tapestry that hung from a wall and held her breath. The crowd of men ran past her, and she relaxed when the sound of their chatter faded into the distance. Then, hearing the sound of children's laughter, she peeked out from behind the tapestry.

The sound was coming from inside the Trophy Room. Elinor-Bear opened the door and gazed up at all the animal heads mounted on the wall. Then she turned and saw the triplets busy assembling a small beast from various animal parts.

The triplets froze. They seemed to know instinctively that the bear was their mother and she'd caught them doing something wrong. The boys stood sheepishly as Elinor roared at them to put the deer head back on the wall where it belonged.

Merida heard the roaring and ran into the Trophy

Room. The triplets stared at Merida quizzically, and she confessed everything in a single breath. "A witch turned Mum into a bear! It's not my fault. We've got to get out of the castle. I need your help."

The triplets' eyes widened with excitement. Merida having turned their mother into a bear was so much better than anything they could put together from parts in the Trophy Room. They couldn't wait to start the adventure!

As Fergus and his men crossed the balcony above the Great Hall, there was a loud roar from within the castle. "Did you hear that?" Lord Dingwall asked.

"Shhh . . . ," Fergus said as he stealthily made his way toward the sound. Suddenly, the shadow of a huge bear appeared on the other side of the Great Hall. "There it goes!" Fergus yelled as the group charged toward it.

The triplets giggled. They were hiding in the corner, manipulating a shadow puppet they had created by holding up a roast chicken from the kitchen. When the boys held it in front of a light, it cast a shadow that looked like a bear! Their dad went roaring after it. When Fergus and his men got near the triplets, the three boys giddily dropped through a trapdoor in the floor. Fergus and his men looked in every direction, confused.

"Maybe we should lay a trap," Lord Dingwall suggested.

"Maybe you should *shut* your trap!" Fergus replied impatiently.

The triplets popped up behind a tapestry and, using the same shadow puppet, led Fergus and his men up the stairs to the roof. After crashing through the door, the men looked around the roof and over the edge of the parapet. Nothing was there.

"It must have sprouted wings," Lord Dingwall said, scratching his bald head.

"A bear in the castle!" Lord Macintosh declared. "It doesn't make sense. It cannot open doors. It's got giant paws."

"Let's just get inside," Fergus said angrily. He yanked at the door and stared at it in disbelief. "It's locked!"

"Dingwall was the last up," MacGuffin said. They all stared accusingly at the squat little Scotsman.

"I propped it open with a stick," he said in his own defense.

On the other side of the door, the triplets smiled as one of them held the stick up and snapped it in two.

Inside the castle kitchen, two maids were attending to Maudie, who was still very frightened. "Oh, for goodness sake, Maudie," one the maids said, and gave her a cup of tea. "Tell us what you saw."

"B-b-b-b—" Maudie answered, her mouth trying to form the word.

Outside the kitchen, Elinor-Bear and Merida were suddenly stopped by one of the triplets. The lad motioned for them to wait until the coast was clear.

Meanwhile, Maudie took a sip of her tea and drew in a breath. "It was a b-b—" she said, but before she could finish, two triplets dropped down the chimney and rolled out, covered in soot. Her nerves already frayed, Maudie didn't know if they were animals or ghosts, and she and the other maids ran shrieking from the kitchen.

Elinor and Merida got the signal from the brother who was peeking through the kitchen door. The coast was clear. "C'mon, Mum . . . quick," Merida said as they slipped into the kitchen. Elinor saw the two soot-covered boys coughing and grumbled her concern.

Merida smiled at the triplets. "They'll be fine. Won't you, boys?" She led her mother to the door. "We've got to hurry now. We don't have much time." As Elinor-Bear squeezed through the door, Merida turned to her brothers. "I'll be back soon," she told them gratefully. "Go on and help yourselves to anything you want as a reward!"

The triplets quickly scurried around the kitchen devouring every sweet in sight . . . including leftover pieces of the small cake Merida had brought to their mother.

20

Up on the castle roof, Fergus and his men decided that the only way to escape was to tie their kilts together to make one long rope and climb down to the ground. Of course, that meant none of them would be wearing a kilt until they had all reached safety. Feeling cold, bare, and grumpier by the minute, the men lowered each other to the castle's main door. "So," Lord Macintosh said as he hopped about, trying to keep warm, "can we get in the door now?"

Fergus stormed up to the main door and tugged on its huge iron ring. To his surprise, it wouldn't open. "It's locked!" he said in disbelief.

Eventually, the men put their kilts back on and hoisted a battering ram to use on the castle door. The whole castle shook with each hit.

Hearing the commotion, Maudie wondered who was banging on the door so hard. "I'm coming!" she called as she waddled down a staircase toward the door. But before she reached it, she noticed a trail of crumbs on the floor.

She looked at the crumbs suspiciously. They led to the kitchen. Maudie quietly pushed the kitchen door open, and just as she'd suspected, there were the triplets, into the sweets again. She saw them gathered around a plate on the floor.

Then the boys turned their faces to her. All three had furry mustaches and patchy little beards. Maudie screamed and ran from the kitchen again. The triplets shrugged and continued eating.

Outside, the men finally smashed the castle door open with the battering ram. "Can we go inside now?" Lord Macintosh asked Fergus. "I'm freezin' my hurdies off!"

Fergus and the lords were about to go in, when Young MacGuffin cried, "Hey! We found the bear!"

"Where?" Fergus shouted excitedly.

Young MacGuffin wheeled out the stuffed bear from the Great Hall. Fergus's face soured as everyone laughed.

"Look!" Lord MacGuffin said, howling. "There *was* a bear in the castle!"

But Fergus knew that underestimating a cagey bear was

no laughing matter. He knew what it was like to have a massive creature threaten his family. He knew how it felt to battle an animal that could bring a man down with one swipe of its paw. He had faced Mor'du, the ferocious demon bear, and he had a wooden leg to prove it.

21

With all the commotion, Merida and Elinor were able to slip away from the castle. Merida knew where they needed to go. The old Witch had created the terrible spell, so surely she could un-create it as well! They needed to find her quickly.

At last, Merida stumbled upon the Ring of Stones once again. She led Elinor to the center of the circle and waited expectantly. Merida looked around. "Where are the will o' the wisps?" she asked anxiously. "We don't have all night." She peered into the misty darkness. "Come out, wisps! Lead me to the Witch's cottage!"

But the stone circle remained dark and silent.

Merida turned to Elinor-Bear, who was grumbling impatiently. "I was standing right here, and the wisp appeared right there!" Merida explained, pointing to the other side of the circle. "Then a whole trail of them led me off into the forest."

Elinor-Bear immediately began to walk in that direction. "So you're just going to head off into the forest and hope we find the Witch, then?" Merida asked, fuming. Her mother didn't answer.

As Merida followed Elinor-Bear through the dark forest, she sensed that her mother was lost. Merida shook her head. "You've no idea where you're going, do you?"

But after stumbling along for some time, Merida suddenly stopped. "Mum!" she exclaimed. "I know this place! We're close. The Witch's cottage should be right over there." She pointed to a small structure in the distance and started running ahead.

Elinor-Bear did her best to keep up, but she moved slowly because she insisted on walking upright. When they finally reached the small cottage, the Witch was gone. The door swung open, revealing an empty room, the cauldron still in the middle.

As they watched, a misty shape formed above the cauldron, arranging itself into the shape of the Witch's face. And it spoke with the Witch's voice: "If you are the red-haired lass, please add the potion on the shelf."

Puzzled, Merida took the powder off the shelf and sprinkled it into the cauldron. Immediately, the cauldron's contents swirled and the Witch spoke again.

"Here's what I forgot to mention, lass," said the misty image. "Your spell will become permanent at the end of the second sunrise . . . unless you remember these words: *Fate be changed, look inside, mend the bond torn by pride!*"

The Witch's face disappeared. "What does that mean?" Merida asked angrily. "A riddle? There's got to be more!"

Desperately, she started dumping other powders and potions into the cauldron. But as she did, the cauldron seemed to overheat, throwing out white smoke everywhere.

When the smoke cleared, Merida and her mother could see that the cottage had crumbled into ruins around them.

Merida dropped to her knees and started digging through the wreckage. "Maybe there's something she left behind. A book of spells or a potion?"

With a panicked look, Elinor-Bear began tearing through the remains of the cottage, too. Huffing and snorting, she picked through broken jars and empty bowls. If the Witch really was gone, Elinor's chances of turning human again were probably gone as well.

Her search became more frantic. She began recklessly tossing debris aside. Then she bumped her head on a ceiling beam that was still attached to the last remaining wall.

"Mum!" Merida called out, hoping Elinor would stop thrashing. "Please!" Elinor-Bear looked into Merida's eyes, and as she did, both her spirit and her body seemed to collapse. She sank to the ground, exhausted.

"There's nothing here," Merida said as rain began to fall on them. She quickly built a tiny fire to keep them warm. "We'll sort it all out tomorrow." She patted Elinor's furry paw, trying to keep her spirits up.

Elinor-Bear nodded absently and curled up in a damp corner of the ruined cottage.

The next morning, Merida woke to the sounds of clinking dishes. She stretched and saw that the rain had stopped. Then she saw her mother wiping off chipped plates and placing them on a table she'd made from the Witch's cauldron.

Elinor-Bear grunted and motioned for Merida to sit at the table. Merida rubbed her eyes. "Uh, good morning?" she said as she sat down and placed her bow on the table. She looked at the berries on the plates. "Sooo, what's all this supposed to be?"

Elinor-Bear attempted to smile and tried to grumble the word "breakfast." Then she grunted at Merida's bow.

Merida didn't understand at first. Then she remembered her manners and put her bow away. Elinor-Bear was pleased and began trying to delicately slice a berry with a twig. The berry shot off her plate and hit Merida in the forehead.

So Elinor-Bear gave up on the twig and daintily ate a berry using her claws. She made a face at the sour taste. Merida nodded. "Found those by the creek, did you?"

Her mother smiled and nodded. "They're nightshade berries," Merida told her. "They're poisonous."

Elinor-Bear spit out the berry and wiped her tongue with a leaf. She grabbed a jug of water and poured some into a teacup. She was drinking it down as Merida looked into the jug and made a face. "Where'd you get this water? It has worms."

Her mother spit out the water and tossed away the cup. Feeling defeated, she dropped her head onto the table and—*Wham!* She sent the tabletop flying over the broken cottage wall.

Merida smiled and confidently threw her bow over her shoulder. "Come on!" she told her mother, and led her to a nearby stream.

Elinor-Bear watched in awe as Merida quickly shot a silvery fish with an arrow. "There you go," Merida said, handing her mother the raw fish. "Breakfast!" Then Merida suddenly took the fish back. "Oh, wait. In your opinion, a princess should not have weapons."

Elinor-Bear put her hands on her hips as if to say, "Hand it over." But as the fish flapped, Elinor shook her head no. Merida crossed her arms. "How do you know you don't like it if you won't try it?"

Merida decided her mother might like the fish cooked, so she roasted it on a spit over a fire. She placed it on a plate and gave it to Elinor.

Elinor roared in delight as she took a taste. Then she made several aggressive growls Merida had never heard before and finished the fish in two big gulps. And just as quickly, the aggressiveness disappeared. She calmed down and patted her mouth with a leaf in a ladylike fashion. She motioned to Merida that she would like more fish.

Merida smiled and pointed to the river. If Elinor-Bear wanted more fish, she would have to get them herself. It was time for the queen to learn a few lessons from Merida.

22

Elinor-Bear followed Merida down to the river's edge. She carefully took off her crown and placed it on the shore. Then she tiptoed into the icy-cold water.

She stood in the stream on her hind legs ... then lunged forward to try to catch the fish swimming upstream. She instantly lost her balance and fell into the cold water. She snapped her jaws at the fish as they swam by but did not catch a single one.

Elinor-Bear roared in frustration, so Merida got down on all fours and demonstrated how to catch fish in her mouth. Merida smiled as her mum gradually got the idea.

It wasn't long before a glistening salmon was flapping in Elinor's mouth. She suddenly seemed to be enjoying herself. She couldn't feel the cold through her thick fur as she began to catch fish after fish, tossing them to Merida on the shore. For the first time, they were working as a team. Merida felt as if the wall that had grown between them was beginning to dissolve, just a bit.

Soon Merida was watching Elinor-Bear sit contentedly in the stream, chewing on a fish. Then, strangely, Elinor turned and ambled out of the river, leaving her crown on the bank. "Hey, where are you going?" Merida said, running after her. "Mum, come back!" Elinor wandered farther and farther away from the river, ignoring Merida completely.

When Merida caught up with her, she reached out and touched Elinor's furry hind leg. Elinor turned. Her eyes were black and cold. Merida could tell her mother didn't recognize her. "Mum?" she asked in shock, backing away.

Elinor began sniffing and moving toward her. "Aah!" Merida cried, and Elinor snapped out of it. She shook her head and the warmth returned to her eyes.

"Mum? Is that you?" Merida asked, still frightened. "You changed. Like you were a . . ."

Elinor-Bear looked at her as if to say, "What are you talking about?"

"Like you were a bear on the *inside*," Merida said.

Elinor-Bear sat down, looking very worried. Merida was worried, too. Suddenly, she saw something that could change everything. "Look!" she cried, and pointed to a small flickering blue light. "A wisp!"

Elinor ran and caught the wisp in her huge paws. She opened them only to see that the wisp had disappeared. Elinor stood on her hind legs, searching for the wisp, when it appeared over her head. But as she reached out and swiped at the little blue light, it darted away. Elinor chased it again and—*BAM!* The wisp led her right into a tree.

Elinor-Bear was holding her head when the wisp appeared again behind her. She spun around and chased the wisp in circles until she finally fell to the ground.

"Jinx cravens hub my bob," Merida said in frustration. Then she sat beside her mum and said soothingly, "Just be still, and listen."

Elinor-Bear's eyes widened as the whispers of many will o' the wisps filled the forest. A trail of wisps materialized, starting right in front of them. "They'll show us the way," Merida told her, and together they followed the trail of flickering blue lights into the mist.

23

As Merida and Elinor-Bear walked deeper into the fog-shrouded forest, Elinor growled her concern. Ahead, a wisp appeared, beckoning them forward. They followed it until, out of the mist, a tall black iron gate loomed over them. Merida noticed a carving on a stone above the gate. It was a double axe, the same symbol that was on the old Witch's ring.

As they passed through the gate, Merida pointed up ahead. "Mum. Look," she said. An ancient ruin of a castle lay in front of them, its rough stone walls nearly sunken into the ground. Elinor groaned nervously.

The remains of the castle stood high on a cliff overlooking a desolate lake ringed by sloping mountains. "I have no idea what this place is," Merida said, confused. She saw the hulls of wrecked ships jutting out on the shore like the broken ribs of some great beast. "Why did the wisps bring us here?"

They picked their way into the ruins and climbed a crumbling staircase within the old castle until they reached the top of its highest tower. Looking down, they saw a large reptilian creature slip into the loch below them. Merida and Elinor-Bear shuddered at the thought of what it might be.

Merida began to investigate the tower. "Whoever lived here," she said as she surveyed the rubble, "they've been gone a long—" But before she could finish, she suddenly fell through the rotted floor.

Merida screamed as she tumbled downward, finally landing on a pile of debris. The wind was knocked out of her, but she was still in one piece. She flipped her hair from her face and looked around.

Light from the hole in the ceiling above her dimly illuminated the old Great Hall of the castle. The room was half caved in. Roots were growing through the walls. Everything was covered in an icy blue frost, and Merida's breath glowed in the light.

Elinor-Bear poked her big head through the hole and grumbled with worry.

"I'm fine, Mum," Merida called up to her. Then she stood and looked around the room. "It's a throne room," she said, gazing at four broken thrones. "You suppose this could have been the kingdom in that story you were telling me? The one with the four princes?"

Merida noticed a huge broken stone tablet with carved figures on it. She counted the figures. There were only three. Then she saw the other piece of the broken carving. Merida gasped. "The fourth!" she said. "The oldest. The willful prince who wanted the strength of ten men!"

Merida ran her hand along the crack in the stone. "Split," she said to herself, "like our tapestry." Merida blinked and remembered in horror the moment she had slashed the tapestry with her sword. She imagined the moment the willful prince had wielded his axe and split the stone. Suddenly, she had a vision of his bearlike face roaring. Merida gasped. "The spell! It's happened before!"

As she backed away from the stone, she heard a crunching under her feet. She looked down to see the bones of men and beasts all over the floor. The stone walls and columns were covered in claw marks.

Merida began breathing hard. "The strength of ten men . . . 'Fate be changed, look inside . . .'" It finally made sense. Her mother's story of the kingdom that fell apart because of a selfish prince, the crossed axes on the Witch's ring . . . It had happened right here. "Oh, no," Merida said as she realized where she was. "The prince became—"

From above, Elinor roared as two red eyes glowed behind Merida. Merida spun around to see a monster of a bear with an elk leg hanging from its mouth. "Mor'du!" she shrieked.

24

Mor'du was every bit the monster of the legends. As he stood on his hind legs, Merida could see he was easily fifteen feet tall and his head was the size of a barrel.

Breathing hard, Merida pulled an arrow from her quiver and shot it. She fired over and over, but Mor'du didn't flinch. He dropped the bloody elk leg from his mouth and charged, swinging his giant paws as he ran. One swipe and he'd tear Merida to pieces.

Merida fell backward. Then, scrambling over a pile of bones, she got to her feet and ran. She jumped out of the monster's way just in time.

Seconds later, Mor'du charged out of the darkness again, roaring and swinging his paws. His claws missed Merida by inches. The crazed bear spun around and charged again.

Merida could see that her arrows were doing no good, and there was no way she could outrun the huge bear. She looked at the ceiling and scrambled up onto a beam. She reached toward the hole, where Elinor-Bear was still looking down in horror.

Finally close enough to see Merida clearly, Elinor-Bear reached in and pulled her up just as Mor'du's head burst through the hole. Elinor saw a large stone and tipped it over into the hole, smashing Mor'du back down into the ruined Great Hall.

Merida wasted no time. She jumped onto her mother's back, and they climbed down from the castle tower and ran full-speed through the heavy mist. Merida now understood where they must go.

Elinor-Bear spotted the Ring of Stones up ahead. She veered off in that direction, running so fast that she nearly hit one of the stones.

"We're back," Merida said when she realized they had reached the circle. "Mum, we have to get to the castle."

Elinor-Bear roared as if to say, "We can't go back there!"

Merida pleaded with her. "If we don't hurry, you might . . ." Merida didn't have the heart to tell her mother that she might become what Mor'du was.

Elinor-Bear nodded.

Merida patted Elinor's big furry head. "I won't let our story end like Mor'du's." she said. She felt sure she knew how to break the spell, and explained to her mother what the key was. "It's the tapestry," Merida said. "'Mend the bond torn by pride.' We have to get back to the castle!"

When Merida and Elinor-Bear reached the edge of the forest, they could see guards perched on the walls of Castle DunBroch. In order to reach the castle, they needed to cross a clearing without being seen. The darkness of the night helped, but Merida waited until she was sure the guards were looking in the other direction.

"Now!" she whispered to Elinor-Bear. The two ran across the clearing to the castle wall. They pressed themselves against it so the guards above couldn't see them. But as they attempted to catch their breath, two guards appeared next to them.

"Bear!" the guards shouted, alerting everyone in the castle. "It's Mor'du!"

Merida and Elinor began to run, trying to return to the safety of the dark forest. Behind them, they could hear the guards shouting, "It's the bear!"

When they reached the cover of the forest, they looked back at the castle. It was flickering with torches as all the guards went on high alert. "We're not going *that* way!"

Merida said, feeling lucky they'd escaped. Then Elinor's head snapped around and Merida found herself suddenly staring into the black, cold eyes of an angry wild animal. Elinor-Bear snarled menacingly at Merida.

Merida let out a little yelp as Elinor-Bear crouched over her. Then she seemed to snap out of it. Merida looked at the hurt expression on her mother's sad face. Elinor-Bear recoiled, horrified by what she'd done.

"It's all right. I'm all right," Merida said. But Elinor-Bear shook her head and ran deeper into the forest. "Mum!" Merida called.

The guards carrying their torches were approaching fast. "Kill the bear!" they shouted.

But when the guards reached the spot where Merida and Elinor-Bear had been standing, mother and daughter had already disappeared. Merida ran through the forest until she caught up with Elinor-Bear. "Mum, stop!" she cried out. "We are going to change you back. We're in this together, aren't we?"

But Elinor-Bear turned away. Merida ran to face her. "You're the queen of DunBroch! You've never given up on anything. My mum has never given up on me! And I promise I'll not give up on you!"

Merida held her mother's face and looked into her eyes

tenderly. "Call me stubborn," Merida said with a small smile. "I get it from you."

Merida's gaze dropped to the ground as she considered their situation. "But it's not going to get us inside the castle," she said.

Elinor-Bear thought for a moment, and then her expression changed. Merida smiled. She knew her mother had an idea.

25

On the castle wall, the guards were still yelling to each other in alarm. "Any sign of him?" one called out. "Check the trees to the north!"

Just below the wall, Merida and Elinor were silently swimming across the castle moat. There was a gate that led from the moat to the castle well. Merida looked at the iron gate and wondered how they might get through. But Elinor-Bear simply ripped the gate off its hinges.

Merida smiled. "Well, that'll do."

In moments, Merida and her mother were peeking out of the well inside the castle. They slowly climbed out. Elinor-Bear shook the water from her fur and followed Merida to the kitchen. They cautiously looked inside, and thankfully, it was empty. "Come on," Merida said.

They passed through the kitchen and into the deserted

hallway. Merida led Elinor to the foot of the stairs that went to the Great Hall. She looked in every direction. "All's clear," she whispered. "Where is everybody?"

Merida and Elinor couldn't have imagined that at a time when the clans thought Mor'du was somewhere nearby, everybody in the castle would be fighting each other instead. But when they peeked into the Great Hall, they saw that tables had been turned into barricades, and axes and arrows were sailing through the air.

"No more talk!" Lord MacGuffin called angrily as he popped up from behind his barricade. "No more traditions! We settle this now!"

Lord Macintosh shouted at Fergus. "You're the king! *You* decide which one of our sons your daughter will marry!" An axe flew through the air and hit his barricade.

"None of your sons are fit to marry my daughter!" Fergus shouted as he glared at them all.

"Then our alliance is over!" Lord Dingwall yelled. "This means war!"

The bagpipes played and the air was suddenly filled with arrows as the clans raged against each other. Merida was shocked. "They're going to murder each other!" she said to Elinor-Bear. "You've got to stop them before it's too late!"

Merida realized Elinor the speech maker could've

stopped them with a single word. But Elinor the bear? She no longer had the ability. Poor Elinor-Bear looked at Merida as if to say, "How can I?"

"I know, I know," Merida said, clutching her hair in panic. "And how do we get through there and up to the Tapestry Room with the lot of them boiling over like that?"

The clans were still going at each other with hammers and axes when a small figure walked into the middle of the brawl. The war cries ceased. It was Merida, and the look on her face was pure conviction.

Fergus looked at her, stunned. "What are you doing, lass?"

"It's all right, Dad," Merida said, doing her best to appear queenly. "I . . . ehm. I have . . . ," she began nervously. She could see surly men from all the clans awaiting her next move. She took a deep breath. "Well, you see . . . I—I have been in conference with the queen."

"Is that so?" Lord Dingwall called out, glaring at her.

"Aye, it is," Merida responded.

"Well, where is she, then?" Lord MacGuffin asked angrily.

Lord Macintosh nodded. "How do we know this isn't some trick?"

Elinor was watching from the shadows. She could hear

the lords' grumbling and protests building.

"Where's the queen?" Lord MacGuffin demanded.

"Aye! Bring her out! We'll not stand for any more of this jiggery-pokery!" Lord Macintosh yelled. The lords all broke into war cries loud enough to nearly rock the walls of the Great Hall.

"*SHUT IT!*" Merida yelled, her voice rising above everyone else's.

The startled lords froze and the Great Hall became dead quiet. Fergus chuckled.

Merida cleared her throat and hoped the right words would come. "Well, I, ah . . . ," she began again, then paused. She looked around and saw that Elinor-Bear had moved out of the shadows and stood at the back of the room.

Lord Macintosh turned to see what Merida was looking at. Elinor quickly froze, posing like one of Fergus's stuffed trophy bears.

Merida kept her eyes on Elinor and began again. "Once there was an ancient kingdom, its name long forgotten."

"What is this?" Lord MacGuffin said, losing patience.

But Merida kept her composure. "That kingdom fell into war, and chaos, and ruin."

Lord Macintosh rolled his eyes and threw up his hands. "Och! We've all heard that tale!"

"Aye," Merida said to him, "but it's true! I know now how one selfish act can turn the fate of a kingdom."

"Bah!" Lord Dingwall said. "It's just a legend."

Merida shook her head confidently. "Legends are lessons. They ring with truths." Elinor recognized the words as her own and beamed with pride as Merida continued. "Our kingdom is young. Our stories are not yet legends, but in them, our bonds were struck. Our clans were once enemies. But when we were threatened from the north, you joined together to defend our lands. You fought for each other."

Merida could see she was starting to get through to them. "You risked everything for each other," she told them. The lords slowly began nodding in agreement.

"Lord MacGuffin, my dad saved your life, stopping an arrow as you ran to Dingwall's aid."

"Aye," Lord MacGuffin said. "And I'll never forget it!"

"And Lord Macintosh. You saved my dad when you charged in on heavy horse and held off the advance."

Macintosh nodded, and Merida looked over to Lord Dingwall. "And we all know how Lord Dingwall broke the enemy line."

"With a mighty throw of his spear!" Lord Macintosh said enthusiastically.

Lord Dingwall turned to Macintosh and said, "Och!

I was aiming at you, ya big tumshie!"

The whole lot broke into riotous laughter as the old warriors remembered times gone by. Merida smiled, too. "The story of this kingdom is a powerful one. My dad rallied your forces, and you made him your king. It was an alliance forged in bravery and friendship, and it lives to this day."

The lords and their clans cheered. Merida waited until they'd quieted down before she continued. "But I've been selfish. I tore a great rift in our bond. There's no one to blame but me. And I know now that I need to amend my mistake and restore our bond.

"And so," Merida said, looking at Elinor, "in the matter of betrothal, I've decided to do what's right and . . ."

Elinor suddenly dropped her stuffed-bear pose and shook her head no. Merida couldn't believe it. She saw Elinor mime "breaking" with her paws. "Uh, and break tradition?" Merida said slowly. Fergus grinned with pride as the lords and their clans considered what Merida was saying.

Elinor looked on lovingly with a paw on her heart. She mimed what she wanted Merida to say for her. "My mother, the queen . . . feels . . . in her heart . . . that I—no, that we—should be free to . . ."

Elinor mimed the words "write" and "book." Merida nodded enthusiastically. "That we should be free to write our own story."

Then Elinor mimed the word "follow" and touched her paw to her heart. "We should follow our hearts," Merida said, "and find love in our own time."

"That's beautiful," Lord Dingwall said, wiping away a tear.

Elinor let out a happy grunt and quickly put her paw over her mouth.

"The queen and I put it to you, then, my lords," She said. "Might our young people decide for themselves who they will love?"

The lords glanced at each other. "What can we say?" Lord Macintosh answered, sounding unsure. "This is . . ."

"A grand idea!" Young Macintosh said to his surprised father. "Give us our say in choosing our own fate!"

Wee Dingwall stepped forward. "Aye! Why shouldn't we choose?"

Lord Dingwall was shocked. "But she's the princess!"

"I didn't pick her out. It was your idea," Wee Dingwall replied defensively.

Lord MacGuffin looked at his son. "And you? You feel the same way?"

Young MacGuffin nodded. "It's not fair making us fight for the hand of a girl who doesn't want any bit of it."

Lord MacGuffin gave his hulk of a son a hug. "That settles it!" Lord MacGuffin announced to the crowd. "Let these lads try and win her heart before they win her hand, if they can!"

Merida grinned as Lord Dingwall stepped forward. "I say the Wee Dingwall has a fighting chance!" he declared.

"Fine by me!" Lord Macintosh laughed. "I'm not the one getting married!" All the lords laughed along with him.

Merida let out a sigh of relief. The disaster had been averted. She looked at her mother and smiled. Elinor beamed as the lords faced Merida and bowed. Fergus placed a hand on his daughter's shoulder. "Just like your mum," he said proudly. "Ye devil!"

Merida smiled, but she still needed to get Elinor-Bear out of the Great Hall before she was discovered. Merida suddenly had an idea, and shouted, "Everyone to the cellar! Let's crack open the king's private reserves to celebrate!"

The crowd cheered and rushed out of the Great Hall. Fergus raised an eyebrow, knowing these rowdy men would drink his cellar dry. He leaned toward a servant. "Psst," he whispered, "bring the tiny glasses."

26

Merida cheerfully escorted the last of the clans from the Great Hall and closed the doors behind them. She was finally able to relax for a moment. She looked at Elinor. They had done it! There'd be no war in the kingdom over her marriage. Merida ran to Elinor and threw her arms around her. They shared a hug for a moment, and then Merida remembered the tapestry.

She and Elinor-Bear easily made their way to the Tapestry Room. Merida looked at the tear she'd created earlier, separating her image from her mother's. She knew she was lucky to have the chance to fix her mistake. "Mend the bond, stitch it up," she said to herself. "We just need needle and thread."

Merida turned to Elinor-Bear. She was sniffing around

a cabinet and knocking things to the floor. "Oh, Mum, not now. Please, not now!" Merida pleaded, realizing Elinor had become a wild bear again. She froze as the black-eyed creature approached and began sniffing her.

At that same moment down the hall, Fergus decided to check on Elinor. She hadn't been feeling well, and he was anxious to tell her the good news about the clans. "Elinor, dear," he said as he entered the room. "You'll never guess who just solved our little suitor problem!"

Fergus was shocked to see the room in shambles. Claw marks were all over the bedposts, and Elinor was gone. Her lovely green dress was on the floor, ripped to shreds.

Fergus burst from the room wild-eyed. "It can't be true! Elinor! Answer me, lass! *Elinoooor!*" he cried as he staggered down the hall, fearing the worst. When he reached the Tapestry Room, he pushed the door open. Fergus saw Merida with a massive bear hovering over her.

Merida saw her father gasp in horror. She rushed to him, crying, "Dad, no! It's not what you think!" But he pushed her aside.

"Get back, Merida," Fergus said angrily as he looked into the cold black eyes of the bear. The bear reared up on its hind legs and bellowed. Fergus drew his sword.

"No! Dad! Don't hurt her!" Merida shouted as Fergus

swung his sword and cut the bear. He circled her, ready to do her in, until the bear roared and swiped him with her paw. Fergus fell to the floor as the bear blinked and her eyes softened.

"Mum!" Merida said, relieved to see her mother's warmth return. But it was too late. Everyone in the castle had already heard the commotion. Merida could hear the lords and their clans entering the Great Hall.

Fergus moaned and slowly began to get up. There was no time to get the tapestry. Merida looked at Elinor, who was stunned and confused. "Mum, run!" she said as she heard the lords racing up the stairs. "*RUN!*"

27

With their swords drawn, the lords burst into the Tapestry Room. "My liege!" Lord Macintosh exclaimed, seeing Fergus lying on the floor. As they rushed to him, the young lords in the hall suddenly came face to face with Elinor-Bear.

"*Bear!*" they shouted as Elinor ran, trying to escape from the castle. With most of the guards still in the Great Hall, Elinor-Bear was able to run out the doors. The castle gate was just ahead.

"Close the gate!" Lord MacGuffin shouted.

Elinor-Bear could see the gate coming down, and she dashed under it just in time.

In the Tapestry Room, Merida ran to her father, who was still struggling to get to his feet. Fergus clutched her shoulders. "Thank your stars, lass. It almost had you! Are you hurt?"

Merida shook her head and desperately tried to explain. "It's mum. It's your wife, Elinor!"

Fergus looked at her as if she were daft. "You're talking nonsense!"

"No, it's the truth. There was a Witch and she gave me a spell! That's not Mor'du!"

Fergus didn't know anything about a witch or a spell. But he did know there was a bear in his castle. "Mor'du or not, I'll avenge your mother. And I'll not risk losing you too!" he said, and stormed out, locking Merida in the Tapestry Room.

Merida knew he'd done it to keep her safe from the bear. She called to him from a small window in the door, still hoping to keep him from making a terrible mistake. "Dad, just listen to me. You can't do this! It's your wife, Elinor!"

As Fergus left, he tossed the key to the Tapestry Room to Maudie at the bottom of the stairs. "Keep this and don't let her out!"

Maudie nodded. "But what about the bear?" she asked, terrified that it might still be near.

"Just stay put!" Fergus replied grimly. He was determined to catch and kill the bear once and for all.

Merida backed away from the door in disbelief. Holding back her tears, she lifted a chair and threw it against the door in frustration. She had to get out somehow. She turned to the fireplace and grabbed a poker. She tried to pry the heavy iron hinges off the door, but they wouldn't budge. Angrily, she raised the poker and beat on the door.

Outside, Fergus and his men were riding through the main gate. "Come on, you sorry bunch of galoots!" Fergus called out, rallying the lords and their clans.

Merida looked out her window and saw the red glow of torches as the men rode into the forest. Elinor wouldn't have a chance. Merida broke the window with the poker and reached out, crying, "Mum! No, no!"

She slumped to the floor in despair. Then she looked up, remembering the tapestry. She realized how to break the spell. She tugged at the tapestry until the whole thing came loose and landed on top of her.

Merida crawled out from under the heavy tapestry, yelling, "Maudie!" She ran to the door and shoved her face as far as she could through the little window. "Maudie! I need you NOW!"

Maudie was huddled at the bottom of the stairs,

clutching the key, too rattled to respond. Merida sensed something else outside the door. She looked down and saw three little bear cubs with pink crumbs on their faces. She knew instantly who they were.

Maudie tried to sneak away but suddenly came face to face with the furry triplets. She let out a small scream and backed away. Then she tucked the key in her bosom and ran!

"Get the key!" Merida yelled to the triplets, and they eagerly chased poor Maudie down the hall. Maudie ran for her life, pushing past two maids who were coming up the stairs.

"Maudie!" one of them exclaimed in surprise. Maudie turned to look at them, but she never slowed down and—
Bam! She ran right into a wall.

As Maudie sat up, the two maids rushed to her aid. They saw terror in Maudie's eyes. Then the shadow of a huge bear suddenly filled the corridor. Maudie and the two maids grabbed their skirts and ran off screaming. The huge shadow shrank as a little cub mischievously stepped into view.

28

Merida waited anxiously in the Tapestry Room for the triplets to return with the key. She could see rain falling outside the window. Merida paced the room, muttering, "Needle and thread . . . needle and thread . . ."

Then she suddenly remembered where she was. She ran to a chest and found it full of sewing supplies. "Och! You beauty!" Merida exclaimed as she picked up a large tapestry needle.

Meanwhile, downstairs, Maudie ran and ran until she reached the kitchen. Panting, she began dragging barrels and wedging them against the door to keep the bears out. She was building the barricade with everything she could find when she stumbled over something.

She looked down and saw two bear cubs standing in

front of her. Maudie gasped and reached for a heavy frying pan. She was about to swat them when she nervously wondered where the third one was. Looking up, she spotted the third cub standing in the rafters. Maudie dropped the frying pan and screamed as the little bear dove out of the rafters and reached into her bosom, where she'd stowed the key!

Upstairs, Merida was busy pushing the needle through the heavy tapestry and tugging at the thread when she heard a cub howl at the door. She looked up and saw a tiny paw holding a key through the Tapestry Room door's window!

Merida gratefully grabbed the key and unlocked the door. The proud triplet cubs were waiting for her in the hall. Merida smiled, and with the tapestry billowing behind her like a heavy cape, she and the cubs raced out to the castle stables.

The rain was falling harder as Merida and the cubs rode Angus into the forest. One of the cubs held the reins while Merida rode at the back, still sewing the tapestry. "Steady, Hamish," she said to the cub who was holding up a lantern to help her see her work.

Together they held on to Angus, hoping to catch up with Fergus and his men before they reached Elinor-Bear.

But the hunting party up ahead was closing in on the bear very fast.

In the blue light of evening, Fergus spotted Elinor-Bear standing just outside the Ring of Stones. Seeing her pursuers, Elinor ran into the center of the circle. "There he goes!" Fergus shouted to the men.

Elinor stumbled and fell. She got up and ran, but when she reached the edge of the circle, she saw men on horseback with spears and arrows. She ran again, darting from one edge of the circle to the other. Finally, she realized she was surrounded.

"Got you!" Lord Macintosh cried as the men began to move in from all sides.

"Back, back!" Lord MacGuffin yelled at Elinor-Bear.

Fergus climbed down from his horse and stepped forward. "Get some light on him!" he shouted. Then he cautioned the hunters, "Any one of you who gets too eager, you'll deal with me!" He wanted the bear for himself.

Merida continued to sew as Angus ran at full speed. "Angus! Easy, laddie!" Merida called out as she struggled to hold on to the tapestry. Her brothers helped keep the tapestry from falling, and they rode on. Then Merida put the last stitch into the tapestry and smiled. "It's done!" she said as Angus suddenly reared up and stopped.

In the mist of the big horse's frozen breath, a tiny blue light appeared. "Aahh!" Merida cried, recognizing the will o' the wisp. Other wisps lit up in a line, forming a path of shimmering lights.

"Hyah!" Merida shouted, urging Angus to follow the wisps' trail.

As Merida, Angus, and the cubs drew closer to the Ring of Stones, the lords were busy tying Elinor-Bear around the neck and staking her to the ground. "Aye, we've got you now!" Lord MacGuffin said, tightening the ropes. "Down you go, you scoundrel!"

Elinor-Bear roared in terror as her body was crisscrossed with heavy ropes. Fergus dismounted his horse and triumphantly stood over the creature. He raised his sword over his head with both hands and plunged it downward.

But before Fergus's sword hit Elinor-Bear, it was deflected by the swift *zing* of an arrow. The lords gasped.

It was Merida. "Get back! That's my mother!" she shouted as she stormed into the circle, still riding Angus. Her bow was in her hand, and she was ready to shoot again.

"Are you out of your mind, lass?" Fergus hollered.

Merida climbed down from Angus and stood between

Fergus and Elinor-Bear. She looked down at Elinor-Bear. "Are you hurt, Mum?"

But before Merida could turn back to Fergus, he shoved her out of the way. Lord Macintosh had his spear against her chest and held her back.

Fergus raised his sword over Elinor again. Merida instantly grabbed Lord Macintosh's spear and flipped him over her shoulder. She grabbed a sword from one of the hunters and ran to her father, blocking his sword with her own.

Merida threw herself in front of Elinor and with one mighty swing cut off Fergus's wooden leg! "I'll not let you kill my mother!" she cried as the triplet cubs ran up and held Fergus to the ground. Fergus began screaming.

"Boys!" Merida said, calling them off.

Fergus looked into the faces of the three little bears. "Boys?" he said in a flash of confused recognition.

But just then, the earthshaking roar of another bear filled the air. "Mor'du!" Merida gasped. The giant bear entered the circle.

Fergus, standing on only one leg, shouted to his men, "Kill it!" But the huge bear just swatted them away. Mor'du grabbed one man in his paws. As his clansmen ran to save him, the great bear knocked the men back against the stones. It set its coal-black eyes on Fergus.

"I'll take you with my bare hands!" Fergus bellowed as Mor'du closed in on him. Mor'du picked up Fergus with his mouth and hurled him into the stones. Then he turned to Merida.

29

Merida stood ready to fire an arrow. But Mor'du merely swatted the bow from her hand. Merida screamed as the huge bear pounced on her, its open mouth inches from her throat.

Then Merida heard the sound of a bear that was even louder than Mor'du. "Mum!" Merida cried as Elinor-Bear, with renewed strength, threw off her ropes and charged Mor'du.

Mor'du turned away from Merida, and the two bears faced off on their hind legs. Elinor-Bear pushed Mor'du away from Merida, and Mor'du hit Elinor-Bear's snout with his huge paw. The two bears growled ferociously as Mor'du shoved Elinor into one of the stones.

Mor'du took Elinor by the neck and bashed her into the

huge stone again. She hit it so hard, the stone cracked. But it gave her an idea.

Elinor-Bear watched as Mor'du turned back to Merida. Elinor kept swatting at Mor'du, trying to bait him. Finally, Mor'du turned and charged her in a fury. At the last moment, Elinor-Bear stepped out of the way and Mor'du slammed into the cracked stone. The ground shuddered as the huge stone toppled and fell onto Mor'du, crushing the bear beneath it.

Elinor and Merida looked up and saw a wisp float up from Mor'du's body. As they watched, the wisp turned into the blue misty figure of a young man, then disappeared. *It's over*, Merida thought. But then she looked at the sewn tapestry and at Elinor, who was still a bear.

"I don't understand," Merida said. "I mended the bond. Why haven't you changed?"

Elinor took the tapestry and threw it over her shoulders, thinking it might help. They both waited expectantly. But nothing happened at all. Merida dropped to her knees, defeated, and began to cry. "Oh, Mum. I'm sorry. This is all my fault. I did this to you. To us. You've always been there for me. You've never given up. I want you back, Mum."

Elinor-Bear growled, and Merida watched in terror as

her mum's eyes turned to the familiar wild-bear black. Merida put her face in her hands and cried as the bear sniffed her. Then Merida threw her arms around the bear's neck and nuzzled its fur. "I love you."

Fergus and his men looked on in shock as the tear in the tapestry that Merida had sewn began to glow and heal. Blue wisps flickered in the air as Merida held her mother tight. Then Merida felt a human hand stroke her hair. She pulled back to see her mother's smiling human face, illuminated by the soft blue light of the wisps. Merida gasped.

Elinor held her daughter and kissed her. "Mum, you've changed," Merida said as she reached out and touched Elinor's cheek.

"No, dear, you did," Elinor replied, and they hugged and laughed.

"Elinor?" Fergus struggled onto his one leg, then pitched himself into a somersault and rolled to them. "*Ha! Haaaa!*" The king howled happily and stood on his one foot. "Oh, Elinor!" He hugged and kissed her.

The lords and their clans gathered around. "Welcome back to your own mortal plane, Your Majesty!" Lord Macintosh said, and the clans cheered heartily. "After this display, I'll be sure never to raise your rancor!"

Elinor smiled, and then she suddenly realized she was wearing nothing but the tapestry wrapped around her. Merida noticed, too, and blushed. "Oh, Mum."

Elinor turned to Fergus with an embarrassed smile and pulled the tapestry tighter around her. "Fergus," she whispered urgently, "don't just stare at me, do something!"

Fergus harrumphed and turned to the lords. "Avert your eyes, lads. Show some respect!" he said loudly. The smiling lords and their clans quickly turned away. They were glad the royal family was back together. Just then, the three naked little triplets came running through the crowd. The boys ran to their family and were quickly pulled into a big hug.

Fergus laughed with pleasure. His family was whole.

The lords, all the clans, and the royal family headed back to the castle. As they left, a small blue wisp drifted up over the stones and disappeared.

ᏜᏜᏜᏜᏜᏜ Epilogue ᏜᏜᏜᏜᏜᏜ

In the castle's Tapestry Room, beside a warm fire, Merida and Queen Elinor were working on a new tapestry together. The tapestry showed Merida and Elinor-Bear facing each other and holding hands. The two were making it so they would always remember what they had learned about themselves and about each other. Elinor would forever value her daughter's courage, and Merida, her mother's wisdom. But most of all, they had learned that the love between them made it possible to overcome every obstacle.

King Fergus entered the room happily and summoned them to see the three lords off. The family made its way to the harbor's edge and waved as the lords' boats pulled away. Suddenly, Fergus noticed that the triplets were absent from the farewell. He looked up and saw the boys clinging to the top of the ships' sails, one on each ship. The wee lads waved as Fergus put his head in his hands. *"How did that happen?"* he said with a sigh. Now he'd have to go and retrieve them.

Shortly afterward, Merida rode Angus over the crest of a hill. And this time, her mother was riding on another horse right behind her. Together they watched the ships sail into the distance. At last, they felt at peace with each other.

As Merida looked out at the ships in the misty harbor, an eagle stretched its wings and flew freely overhead. The princess laughed and let her wild red hair blow in the breeze. Yes, someday she would likely marry and become queen of DunBroch, but that would be another story.